# SIDDHARTHA
# AN INDIAN TALE

# SIDDHARTHA

## AN INDIAN TALE

By

**HERMANN HESSE**

GYAN

ISBN : 978-81-212-1511-4(HB)

First Published, 1922

Published, 2018

*Published by*

Gyan Publishing House
5, Ansari Road
Daryaganj, New Delhi-110002
Phone: 011-47034999, 9811692060
www.gyanbooks.com
E-mail: books@gyanbooks.com

*Printed at:* G. Print Process, Delhi.

# Contents

# FIRST PART

**To Romain Rolland, my dear friend**

## THE SON OF THE BRAHMAN

In the shade of the house, in the sunshine of the riverbank near the boats, in the shade of the Sal-wood forest, in the shade of the fig tree is where Siddhartha grew up, the handsome son of the Brahman, the young falcon, together with his friend Govinda, son of a Brahman. The sun tanned his light shoulders by the banks of the river when bathing, performing the sacred ablutions, the sacred offerings. In the mango grove, shade poured into his black eyes, when playing as a boy, when his mother sang, when the sacred offerings were made, when his father, the scholar, taught him, when the wise men talked. For a long time, Siddhartha had been partaking in the discussions of the wise men, practising debate with Govinda, practising with Govinda the art of reflection, the service of meditation. He already knew how to speak the Om silently, the word of words, to speak it silently into himself while inhaling, to speak it silently out of himself while exhaling, with all the concentration of his soul, the forehead surrounded by the glow of the clear-thinking spirit. He already knew to feel Atman in the depths of his being, indestructible, one with the universe.

Joy leapt in his father's heart for his son who was quick to learn, thirsty for knowledge; he saw him growing up to become great wise man and priest, a prince among the Brahmans.

Bliss leapt in his mother's breast when she saw him, when she saw him walking, when she saw him sit down and get up, Siddhartha, strong, handsome, he who was walking on slender legs, greeting her with perfect respect.

Love touched the hearts of the Brahmans' young daughters when Siddhartha walked through the lanes of the town with the luminous forehead, with the eye of a king, with his slim hips.

But more than all the others he was loved by Govinda, his friend, the son of a Brahman. He loved Siddhartha's eye and sweet voice, he loved his walk and the perfect decency of his movements, he loved everything Siddhartha did and said and what he loved most was his spirit, his transcendent, fiery thoughts, his ardent will, his high calling. Govinda knew: he would not become a common Brahman, not a lazy official in charge of offerings; not a greedy merchant with magic spells; not a vain, vacuous speaker; not a mean, deceitful priest; and also not a decent, stupid sheep in the herd of the many. No, and he, Govinda, as well did not want to become one of those, not one of those tens of thousands of Brahmans. He wanted to follow Siddhartha, the beloved, the splendid. And in days to come, when Siddhartha would become a god, when he would join the glorious, then Govinda wanted to follow him as his friend, his companion, his servant, his spear-carrier, his shadow.

Siddhartha was thus loved by everyone. He was a source of joy for everybody, he was a delight for them all.

But he, Siddhartha, was not a source of joy for himself, he found no delight in himself. Walking the rosy paths of the fig tree garden, sitting in the bluish shade of the grove of contemplation, washing his limbs daily in the bath of repentance, sacrificing in the dim shade of the mango forest, his gestures of perfect decency, everyone's love and joy, he still lacked all joy in his heart. Dreams and restless thoughts came into his mind, flowing from the water of the river, sparkling from the stars of the night, melting from the beams of the sun, dreams came to him and a restlessness of the soul, fuming from the sacrifices, breathing forth from the verses of the Rig-Veda, being infused into him, drop by drop, from the teachings of the old Brahmans.

Siddhartha had started to nurse discontent in himself, he had started to feel that the love of his father and the love of his mother, and also the love of his friend, Govinda, would not bring him joy for ever and ever, would not nurse him, feed him, satisfy him. He had started to suspect that his venerable father and his other teachers, that the wise Brahmans had already revealed to him the most and best of their wisdom, that they had already filled his expecting vessel with their richness, and the vessel was not full, the spirit was not content, the soul was not calm, the heart was not satisfied. The ablutions were good, but they were water, they did not wash off the sin, they did not heal the spirit's thirst, they did not relieve the fear in his heart. The sacrifices and the invocation of the gods were excellent—but was that all? Did the sacrifices give a happy fortune? And what about the gods? Was it really Prajapati who had created the world? Was it not the Atman, He, the only one, the singular one? Were the gods not creations, created like me and you, subject to time, mortal? Was it therefore good, was it right, was it meaningful and the highest occupation to make offerings to the gods? For whom else were offerings to be made, who else was to be worshipped but Him, the only one, the Atman? And where was Atman to be found, where did He reside, where did his eternal heart beat, where else but in one's own self, in its innermost part, in its indestructible part, which everyone had in himself? But where, where was this self, this innermost part, this ultimate part? It was not flesh and bone, it was neither thought nor consciousness, thus the wisest ones taught. So, where, where was it? To reach this place, the self, myself, the Atman, there was another way, which was worthwhile looking for? Alas, and nobody showed this way, nobody knew it, not the father, and not the teachers and wise men, not the holy sacrificial songs! They knew everything, the Brahmans and their holy books, they knew everything, they had taken care of everything and of more than everything, the creation of the world, the origin of speech, of food, of inhaling, of exhaling, the arrangement of the senses, the acts of the gods, they knew infinitely much—but was it valuable to know all of this, not knowing that one and only thing, the most important thing, the solely important thing?

Surely, many verses of the holy books, particularly in the Upanishades of Samaveda, spoke of this innermost and ultimate thing, wonderful verses. "Your soul is the whole world", was written there, and it was written that man in his sleep, in his deep sleep, would meet with his innermost part and would reside in the Atman. Marvellous wisdom was in these verses, all knowledge of the wisest ones had been collected here in magic words, pure as honey collected by bees. No, not to be looked down upon was the tremendous amount of enlightenment which lay here collected and preserved by innumerable generations of wise Brahmans.— But where were the Brahmans, where the priests, where the wise men or penitents, who had succeeded in not just knowing this deepest of all knowledge but also to live it? Where was the knowledgeable one who wove his spell to bring his familiarity with the Atman out of the sleep into the state of being awake, into the life, into every step of the way, into word and deed? Siddhartha knew many venerable Brahmans, chiefly his father, the pure one, the scholar, the most venerable one. His father was to be admired, quiet and noble were his manners, pure his life, wise his words, delicate and noble thoughts lived behind its brow —but even he, who knew so much, did he live in blissfulness, did he have peace, was he not also just a searching man, a thirsty man? Did he not, again and again, have to drink from holy sources, as a thirsty man, from the offerings, from the books, from the disputes of the Brahmans? Why did he, the irreproachable one, have to wash off sins every day, strive for a cleansing every day, over and over every day? Was not Atman in him, did not the pristine source spring from his heart? It had to be found, the pristine source in one's own self, it had to be possessed! Everything else was searching, was a detour, was getting lost.

Thus were Siddhartha's thoughts, this was his thirst, this was his suffering.

Often he spoke to himself from a Chandogya-Upanishad the words: "Truly, the name of the Brahman is satyam—verily, he who knows such a thing, will enter the heavenly world every day." Often, it seemed near, the heavenly world, but never he had reached it completely, never he had quenched the ultimate thirst. And among all the wise and wisest men, he knew and whose instructions he had received, among all of them there was no one, who had reached it completely, the heavenly world, who had quenched it completely, the eternal thirst.

"Govinda," Siddhartha spoke to his friend, "Govinda, my dear, come with me under the Banyan tree, let's practise meditation."

They went to the Banyan tree, they sat down, Siddhartha right here, Govinda twenty paces away. While putting himself down, ready to speak the Om, Siddhartha repeated murmuring the verse:

Om is the bow, the arrow is soul, The Brahman is the arrow's target, That one should incessantly hit.

After the usual time of the exercise in meditation had passed, Govinda rose. The evening had come, it was time to perform the evening's ablution. He called Siddhartha's name. Siddhartha did not answer. Siddhartha sat there lost in thought, his eyes were rigidly focused towards a very distant target, the tip of his tongue was protruding a little between the teeth, he seemed not to breathe. Thus sat he, wrapped up in contemplation, thinking Om, his soul sent after the Brahman as an arrow.

Once, Samanas had travelled through Siddhartha's town, ascetics on a pilgrimage, three skinny, withered men, neither old nor young, with dusty and bloody shoulders, almost naked, scorched by the sun, surrounded by loneliness, strangers and enemies to the world, strangers and lank jackals in the realm of humans. Behind them blew a hot scent of quiet passion, of destructive service, of merciless self-denial.

In the evening, after the hour of contemplation, Siddhartha spoke to Govinda: "Early tomorrow morning, my friend, Siddhartha will go to the Samanas. He will become a Samana."

Govinda turned pale, when he heard these words and read the decision in the motionless face of his friend, unstoppable like the arrow shot from the bow. Soon and with the first glance, Govinda realized: Now it is beginning, now Siddhartha is taking his own way, now his fate is beginning to sprout, and with his, my own. And he turned pale like a dry banana-skin.

"O Siddhartha," he exclaimed, "will your father permit you to do that?"

Siddhartha looked over as if he was just waking up. Arrow-fast he read in Govinda's soul, read the fear, read the submission.

"O Govinda," he spoke quietly, "let's not waste words. Tomorrow, at daybreak I will begin the life of the Samanas. Speak no more of it."

Siddhartha entered the chamber, where his father was sitting on a mat of bast, and stepped behind his father and remained standing there, until his father felt that someone was standing behind him. Quoth the Brahman: "Is that you, Siddhartha? Then say what you came to say."

Quoth Siddhartha: "With your permission, my father. I came to tell you that it is my longing to leave your house tomorrow and go to the ascetics. My desire is to become a Samana. May my father not oppose this."

The Brahman fell silent, and remained silent for so long that the stars in the small window wandered and changed their relative positions, 'ere the silence was broken. Silent and motionless stood the son with his arms folded, silent and motionless sat the father on the mat, and the stars traced their paths in the sky. Then spoke the father: "Not proper it is for a Brahman to speak harsh and angry words. But indignation is in my heart. I wish not to hear this request for a second time from your mouth."

Slowly, the Brahman rose; Siddhartha stood silently, his arms folded.

"What are you waiting for?" asked the father.

Quoth Siddhartha: "You know what."

Indignant, the father left the chamber; indignant, he went to his bed and lay down.

After an hour, since no sleep had come over his eyes, the Brahman stood up, paced to and fro, and left the house. Through the small window of the chamber he looked back inside, and there he saw Siddhartha standing, his arms folded, not moving from his spot. Pale shimmered his bright robe. With anxiety in his heart, the father returned to his bed.

After another hour, since no sleep had come over his eyes, the Brahman stood up again, paced to and fro, walked out of the house and saw that the moon had risen. Through the window of the chamber he looked back inside; there stood Siddhartha, not moving from his spot, his arms folded, moonlight reflecting from his bare shins. With worry in his heart, the father went back to bed.

And he came back after an hour, he came back after two hours, looked through the small window, saw Siddhartha standing, in the moon light, by the light of the stars, in the darkness. And he came back hour after hour, silently, he looked into the chamber, saw him standing in the same place, filled his heart with anger, filled his heart with unrest, filled his heart with anguish, filled it with sadness.

And in the night's last hour, before the day began, he returned, stepped into the room, saw the young man standing there, who seemed tall and like a stranger to him.

"Siddhartha," he spoke, "what are you waiting for?"

"You know what."

"Will you always stand that way and wait, until it'll becomes morning, noon, and evening?"

"I will stand and wait.

"You will become tired, Siddhartha."

"I will become tired."

"You will fall asleep, Siddhartha."

"I will not fall asleep."

"You will die, Siddhartha."

"I will die."

"And would you rather die, than obey your father?"

"Siddhartha has always obeyed his father."

"So will you abandon your plan?"

"Siddhartha will do what his father will tell him to do."

The first light of day shone into the room. The Brahman saw that Siddhartha was trembling softly in his knees. In Siddhartha's face he saw no trembling, his eyes were fixed on a distant spot. Then his father realized that even now Siddhartha no longer dwelt with him in his home, that he had already left him.

The Father touched Siddhartha's shoulder.

"You will," he spoke, "go into the forest and be a Samana. When you'll have found blissfulness in the forest, then come back and teach me to be blissful. If you'll find disappointment, then return and let us once again make offerings to the gods together. Go now and kiss your mother, tell her where you are going to. But for me it is time to go to the river and to perform the first ablution."

He took his hand from the shoulder of his son and went outside. Siddhartha wavered to the side, as he tried to walk. He put his limbs back under control, bowed to his father, and went to his mother to do as his father had said.

As he slowly left on stiff legs in the first light of day the still quiet town, a shadow rose near the last hut, who had crouched there, and joined the pilgrim—Govinda.

"You have come," said Siddhartha and smiled.

"I have come," said Govinda.

# WITH THE SAMANAS

In the evening of this day they caught up with the ascetics, the skinny Samanas, and offered them their companionship and—obedience. They were accepted.

Siddhartha gave his garments to a poor Brahman in the street. He wore nothing more than the loincloth and the earth-coloured, unsown cloak. He ate only once a day, and never something cooked. He fasted for fifteen days. He fasted for twenty-eight days. The flesh waned from his thighs and cheeks. Feverish dreams flickered from his enlarged eyes, long nails grew slowly on his parched fingers and a dry, shaggy beard grew on his chin. His glance turned to ice when he encountered women; his mouth twitched with contempt, when he walked through a city of nicely dressed people. He saw merchants trading, princes hunting, mourners wailing for their dead, whores offering themselves, physicians trying to help the sick, priests determining the most suitable day for seeding, lovers loving, mothers nursing their children—and all of this was not worthy of one look from his eye, it all lied, it all stank, it all stank of lies, it all pretended to be meaningful and joyful and beautiful, and it all was just concealed putrefaction. The world tasted bitter. Life was torture.

A goal stood before Siddhartha, a single goal: to become empty, empty of thirst, empty of wishing, empty of dreams, empty of joy and sorrow. Dead to himself, not to be a self any more, to find tranquility with an emptied heard, to be open to miracles in unselfish thoughts, that was his goal. Once all of my self was overcome and had died, once every desire and every urge was silent in the heart, then the ultimate part of me had to awake, the innermost of my being, which is no longer my self, the great secret.

Silently, Siddhartha exposed himself to burning rays of the sun directly above, glowing with pain, glowing with thirst, and stood there, until he neither felt any pain nor thirst any more. Silently, he stood there in the rainy season, from his hair the water was dripping over freezing shoulders, over freezing hips and legs, and the penitent stood there, until he could not feel the cold in his shoulders and legs any more, until they were silent, until they were quiet. Silently, he cowered in the thorny bushes, blood dripped from the burning skin, from festering wounds dripped pus, and Siddhartha stayed rigidly, stayed motionless, until no blood flowed any more, until nothing stung any more, until nothing burned any more.

Siddhartha sat upright and learned to breathe sparingly, learned to get along with only few breathes, learned to stop breathing. He learned, beginning with the breath, to calm the beat of his heart, leaned to reduce the beats of his heart, until they were only a few and almost none.

Instructed by the oldest if the Samanas, Siddhartha practised self-denial, practised meditation, according to a new Samana rules. A heron flew over the bamboo forest—and Siddhartha accepted the heron into his soul, flew over forest and mountains, was a heron, ate fish, felt the pangs of a heron's hunger, spoke the heron's croak, died a heron's death. A dead jackal was lying on the sandy bank, and Siddhartha's soul slipped inside the body, was the dead jackal, lay on the banks, got bloated, stank, decayed, was dismembered by hyaenas, was skinned by vultures, turned into a skeleton, turned to dust, was blown across the fields. And Siddhartha's soul returned, had died, had decayed, was scattered as dust, had tasted the gloomy intoxication of the cycle, awaited in new thirst like a hunter in the gap, where he could escape from the cycle, where the end of the causes, where an eternity without suffering began. He killed his senses, he killed his memory, he slipped out of his self into thousands of other forms, was an animal, was carrion, was stone, was wood, was water, and awoke every time to find his old self again, sun shone or moon, was his self again, turned round in the cycle, felt thirst, overcame the thirst, felt new thirst.

Siddhartha learned a lot when he was with the Samanas, many ways leading away from the self he learned to go. He went the way of self-denial by means of pain, through voluntarily suffering and overcoming pain, hunger, thirst, tiredness. He went the way of self-denial by means of meditation, through imagining the mind to be void of all conceptions. These and other ways he learned to go, a thousand times he left his self, for hours and days he remained in the non-self. But though the ways led away from the self, their end nevertheless always led back to the self. Though Siddhartha fled from the self a thousand times, stayed in nothingness, stayed in the animal, in the stone, the return was inevitable, inescapable was the hour, when he found himself back in the sunshine or in the moonlight, in the shade or in the rain, and was once again his self and Siddhartha, and again felt the agony of the cycle which had been forced upon him.

By his side lived Govinda, his shadow, walked the same paths, undertook the same efforts. They rarely spoke to one another, than the service and the exercises required. Occasionally the two of them went through the villages, to beg for food for themselves and their teachers.

"How do you think, Govinda," Siddhartha spoke one day while begging this way, "how do you think did we progress? Did we reach any goals?"

Govinda answered: "We have learned, and we'll continue learning. You'll be a great Samana, Siddhartha. Quickly, you've learned every exercise, often the old Samanas have admired you. One day, you'll be a holy man, oh Siddhartha."

Quoth Siddhartha: "I can't help but feel that it is not like this, my friend. What I've learned, being among the Samanas, up to this day, this, oh Govinda, I could have learned more quickly and by simpler means. In every tavern of that part of a town where the whorehouses are, my friend, among carters and gamblers I could have learned it."

Quoth Govinda: "Siddhartha is putting me on. How could you have learned meditation, holding your breath, insensitivity against hunger and pain there among these wretched people?"

And Siddhartha said quietly, as if he was talking to himself: "What is meditation? What is leaving one's body? What is fasting? What is holding one's breath? It is fleeing from the self, it is a short escape of the agony of being a self, it is a short numbing of the senses against the pain and the pointlessness of life. The same escape, the same short numbing is what the driver of an ox-cart finds in the inn, drinking a few bowls of rice-wine or fermented coconut-milk. Then he won't feel his self any more, then he won't feel the pains of life any more, then he finds a short numbing of the senses. When he falls asleep over his bowl of rice-wine, he'll find the same what Siddhartha and Govinda find when they escape their bodies through long exercises, staying in the non-self. This is how it is, oh Govinda."

Quoth Govinda: "You say so, oh friend, and yet you know that Siddhartha is no driver of an ox-cart and a Samana is no drunkard. It's true that a drinker numbs his senses, it's true that he briefly escapes and rests, but he'll return from the delusion, finds everything to be unchanged, has not become wiser, has gathered no enlightenment,—has not risen several steps."

And Siddhartha spoke with a smile: "I do not know, I've never been a drunkard. But that I, Siddhartha, find only a short numbing of the senses in my exercises and meditations and that I am just as far removed from wisdom, from salvation, as a child in the mother's womb, this I know, oh Govinda, this I know."

And once again, another time, when Siddhartha left the forest together with Govinda, to beg for some food in the village for their brothers and teachers, Siddhartha began to speak and said: "What now, oh Govinda, might we be on the right path? Might we get closer to enlightenment? Might we get closer to salvation? Or do we perhaps live in a circle— we, who have thought we were escaping the cycle?"

Quoth Govinda: "We have learned a lot, Siddhartha, there is still much to learn. We are not going around in circles, we are moving up, the circle is a spiral, we have already ascended many a level."

Siddhartha answered: "How old, would you think, is our oldest Samana, our venerable teacher?"

Quoth Govinda: "Our oldest one might be about sixty years of age."

And Siddhartha: "He has lived for sixty years and has not reached the nirvana. He'll turn seventy and eighty, and you and me, we will grow just as old and will do our exercises, and will fast, and will meditate. But we will not reach the nirvana, he won't and we won't. Oh Govinda, I believe out of all the Samanas out there, perhaps not a single one, not a single one, will reach the nirvana. We find comfort, we find numbness, we learn feats, to deceive others. But the most important thing, the path of paths, we will not find."

"If you only," spoke Govinda, "wouldn't speak such terrible words, Siddhartha! How could it be that among so many learned men, among so many Brahmans, among so many austere and venerable Samanas, among so many who are searching, so many who are eagerly trying, so many holy men, no one will find the path of paths?"

But Siddhartha said in a voice which contained just as much sadness as mockery, with a quiet, a slightly sad, a slightly mocking voice: "Soon, Govinda, your friend will leave the path of the Samanas, he has walked along your side for so long. I'm suffering of thirst, oh Govinda, and on this long path of a Samana, my thirst has remained as strong as ever. I always thirsted for knowledge, I have always been full of questions. I have asked the Brahmans, year after year, and I have asked the holy Vedas, year after year, and I have asked the devote Samanas, year after year. Perhaps, oh Govinda, it had been just as well, had been just as smart and just as profitable, if I had asked the hornbill-bird or the chimpanzee. It took me a long time and am not finished learning this yet, oh Govinda: that there is nothing to be learned! There is indeed no such thing, so I believe, as what we refer to as `learning'. There is, oh my friend, just one knowledge, this is everywhere, this is Atman, this is within me and within you and within every creature. And so I'm starting to believe that this knowledge has no worser enemy than the desire to know it, than learning."

At this, Govinda stopped on the path, rose his hands, and spoke: "If you, Siddhartha, only would not bother your friend with this kind of talk! Truly, you words stir up fear in my heart. And just consider: what would become of the sanctity of prayer, what of the venerability of the Brahmans' caste, what of the holiness of the Samanas, if it was as you say, if there was no learning?! What, oh Siddhartha, what would then become of all of this what is holy, what is precious, what is venerable on earth?!"

And Govinda mumbled a verse to himself, a verse from an Upanishad:

He who ponderingly, of a purified spirit, loses himself in the meditation of Atman, unexpressable by words is his blissfulness of his heart.

But Siddhartha remained silent. He thought about the words which Govinda had said to him and thought the words through to their end.

Yes, he thought, standing there with his head low, what would remain of all that which seemed to us to be holy? What remains? What can stand the test? And he shook his head.

At one time, when the two young men had lived among the Samanas for about three years and had shared their exercises, some news, a rumour, a myth reached them after being retold many times: A man had appeared, Gotama by name, the exalted one, the Buddha, he had overcome the suffering of the world in himself and had halted the cycle of rebirths. He was said to wander through the land, teaching, surrounded by disciples, without possession, without home, without a wife, in the yellow cloak of an ascetic, but with a cheerful brow, a man of bliss, and Brahmans and princes would bow down before him and would become his students.

This myth, this rumour, this legend resounded, its fragrants rose up, here and there; in the towns, the Brahmans spoke of it and in the forest, the Samanas; again and again, the name of Gotama, the Buddha reached the ears of the young men, with good and with bad talk, with praise and with defamation.

It was as if the plague had broken out in a country and news had been spreading around that in one or another place there was a man, a wise man, a knowledgeable one, whose word and breath was enough to heal everyone who had been infected with the pestilence, and as such news would go through the land and everyone would talk about it, many would believe, many would doubt, but many would get on their way as soon as possible, to seek the wise man, the helper, just like this this myth ran through the land, that fragrant myth of Gotama, the Buddha, the wise man of the family of Sakya. He possessed, so the believers said, the highest enlightenment, he remembered his previous lives, he had reached the nirvana and never returned into the cycle, was never again submerged in the murky river of physical forms. Many wonderful and unbelievable things were reported of him, he had performed miracles, had overcome the devil, had spoken to the gods. But his enemies and disbelievers said, this Gotama was a vain seducer, he would spent his days in luxury, scorned the offerings, was without learning, and knew neither exercises nor self-castigation.

The myth of Buddha sounded sweet. The scent of magic flowed from these reports. After all, the world was sick, life was hard to bear—and behold, here a source seemed to spring forth, here a messenger seemed to call out, comforting, mild, full of noble promises. Everywhere where the rumour of Buddha was heard, everywhere in the lands of India, the young men listened up, felt a longing, felt hope, and among the Brahmans' sons of the towns and villages every pilgrim and stranger was welcome, when he brought news of him, the exalted one, the Sakyamuni.

The myth had also reached the Samanas in the forest, and also Siddhartha, and also Govinda, slowly, drop by drop, every drop laden with hope, every drop laden with doubt. They rarely talked about it, because the oldest one of the Samanas did not like this myth. He had heard that this alleged Buddha used to be an ascetic before and had lived in the forest, but had then turned back to luxury and worldly pleasures, and he had no high opinion of this Gotama.

"Oh Siddhartha," Govinda spoke one day to his friend. "Today, I was in the village, and a Brahman invited me into his house, and in his house, there was the son of a Brahman from Magadha, who has seen the Buddha with his own eyes and has heard him teach. Verily, this made my chest ache when I breathed, and thought to myself: If only I would too, if only we both would too, Siddhartha and me, live to see the hour when we will hear the teachings from the mouth of this perfected man! Speak, friend, wouldn't we want to go there too and listen to the teachings from the Buddha's mouth?"

Quoth Siddhartha: "Always, oh Govinda, I had thought, Govinda would stay with the Samanas, always I had believed his goal was to live to be sixty and seventy years of age and to keep on practising those feats and exercises, which are becoming a Samana. But behold, I had not known Govinda well enough, I knew little of his heart. So now you, my faithful friend, want to take a new path and go there, where the Buddha spreads his teachings."

Quoth Govinda: "You're mocking me. Mock me if you like, Siddhartha! But have you not also developed a desire, an eagerness, to hear these teachings? And have you not at one time said to me, you would not walk the path of the Samanas for much longer?"

At this, Siddhartha laughed in his very own manner, in which his voice assumed a touch of sadness and a touch of mockery, and said: "Well, Govinda, you've spoken well, you've remembered correctly. If you only remembered the other thing as well, you've heard from me, which is that I have grown distrustful and tired against teachings and learning, and that my faith in words, which are brought to us by teachers, is small. But let's do it, my dear, I am willing to listen to these teachings—though in my heart I believe that we've already tasted the best fruit of these teachings."

Quoth Govinda: "Your willingness delights my heart. But tell me, how should this be possible? How should the Gotama's teachings, even before we have heard them, have already revealed their best fruit to us?"

Quoth Siddhartha: "Let us eat this fruit and wait for the rest, oh Govinda! But this fruit, which we already now received thanks to the Gotama, consisted in him calling us away from the Samanas! Whether he has also other and better things to give us, oh friend, let us await with calm hearts."

On this very same day, Siddhartha informed the oldest one of the Samanas of his decision, that he wanted to leave him. He informed the oldest one with all the courtesy and modesty becoming to a younger one and a student. But the Samana became angry, because the two young men wanted to leave him, and talked loudly and used crude swearwords.

Govinda was startled and became embarrassed. But Siddhartha put his mouth close to Govinda's ear and whispered to him: "Now, I want to show the old man that I've learned something from him."

Positioning himself closely in front of the Samana, with a concentrated soul, he captured the old man's glance with his glances, deprived him of his power, made him mute, took away his free will, subdued him under his own will, commanded him, to do silently, whatever he demanded him to do. The old man became mute, his eyes became motionless, his will was paralysed, his arms were hanging down; without power, he had fallen victim to Siddhartha's spell. But Siddhartha's thoughts brought the Samana under their control, he had to carry out, what they commanded. And thus, the old man made several bows, performed gestures of blessing, spoke stammeringly a godly wish for a good journey. And the young men returned the bows with thanks, returned the wish, went on their way with salutations.

On the way, Govinda said: "Oh Siddhartha, you have learned more from the Samanas than I knew. It is hard, it is very hard to cast a spell on an old Samana. Truly, if you had stayed there, you would soon have learned to walk on water."

"I do not seek to walk on water," said Siddhartha. "Let old Samanas be content with such feats!"

## GOTAMA

In the town of Savathi, every child knew the name of the exalted Buddha, and every house was prepared to fill the alms-dish of Gotama's disciples, the silently begging ones. Near the town was Gotama's favourite place to stay, the grove of Jetavana, which the rich merchant Anathapindika, an obedient worshipper of the exalted one, had given him and his people for a gift.

All tales and answers, which the two young ascetics had received in their search for Gotama's abode, had pointed them towards this area. And arriving at Savathi, in the very first house, before the door of which they stopped to beg, food has been offered to them, and they accepted the food, and Siddhartha asked the woman, who handed them the food:

"We would like to know, oh charitable one, where the Buddha dwells, the most venerable one, for we are two Samanas from the forest and have come, to see him, the perfected one, and to hear the teachings from his mouth."

Quoth the woman: "Here, you have truly come to the right place, you Samanas from the forest. You should know, in Jetavana, in the garden of Anathapindika is where the exalted one dwells. There you pilgrims shall spent the night, for there is enough space for the innumerable, who flock here, to hear the teachings from his mouth."

This made Govinda happy, and full of joy he exclaimed: "Well so, thus we have reached our destination, and our path has come to an end! But tell us, oh mother of the pilgrims, do you know him, the Buddha, have you seen him with your own eyes?"

Quoth the woman: "Many times I have seen him, the exalted one. On many days, I have seen him, walking through the alleys in silence, wearing his yellow cloak, presenting his alms-dish in silence at the doors of the houses, leaving with a filled dish."

Delightedly, Govinda listened and wanted to ask and hear much more. But Siddhartha urged him to walk on. They thanked and left and hardly had to ask for directions, for rather many pilgrims and monks as well from Gotama's community were on their way to the Jetavana. And since they reached it at night, there were constant arrivals, shouts, and talk of those who sought shelter and got it. The two Samanas, accustomed to life in the forest, found quickly and without making any noise a place to stay and rested there until the morning.

At sunrise, they saw with astonishment what a large crowd of believers and curious people had spent the night here. On all paths of the marvellous grove, monks walked in yellow robes, under the trees they sat here and there, in deep contemplation—or in a conversation about spiritual matters, the shady gardens looked like a city, full of people, bustling like bees. The majority of the monks went out with their alms-dish, to collect food in town for their lunch, the only meal of the day. The Buddha himself, the enlightened one, was also in the habit of taking this walk to beg in the morning.

Siddhartha saw him, and he instantly recognised him, as if a god had pointed him out to him. He saw him, a simple man in a yellow robe, bearing the alms-dish in his hand, walking silently.

"Look here!" Siddhartha said quietly to Govinda. "This one is the Buddha."

Attentively, Govinda looked at the monk in the yellow robe, who seemed to be in no way different from the hundreds of other monks. And soon, Govinda also realized: This is the one. And they followed him and observed him.

The Buddha went on his way, modestly and deep in his thoughts, his calm face was neither happy nor sad, it seemed to smile quietly and inwardly. With a hidden smile, quiet, calm, somewhat resembling a healthy child, the Buddha walked, wore the robe and placed his feet just as all of his monks did, according to a precise rule. But his face and his walk, his quietly lowered glance, his quietly dangling hand and even every finger of his quietly dangling hand expressed peace, expressed perfection, did not search, did not imitate, breathed softly in an unwhithering calm, in an unwhithering light, an untouchable peace.

Thus Gotama walked towards the town, to collect alms, and the two Samanas recognised him solely by the perfection of his calm, by the quietness of his appearance, in which there was no searching, no desire, no imitation, no effort to be seen, only light and peace.

"Today, we'll hear the teachings from his mouth." said Govinda.

Siddhartha did not answer. He felt little curiosity for the teachings, he did not believe that they would teach him anything new, but he had, just as Govinda had, heard the contents of this Buddha's teachings again and again, though these reports only represented second- or third-hand information. But attentively he looked at Gotama's head, his shoulders, his feet, his quietly dangling hand, and it seemed to him as if every joint of every finger of this hand was of these teachings, spoke of, breathed of, exhaled the fragrant of, glistened of truth. This man, this Buddha was truthful down to the gesture of his last finger. This man was holy. Never before, Siddhartha had venerated a person so much, never before he had loved a person as much as this one.

They both followed the Buddha until they reached the town and then returned in silence, for they themselves intended to abstain from on this day. They saw Gotama returning—what he ate could not even have satisfied a bird's appetite, and they saw him retiring into the shade of the mango-trees.

But in the evening, when the heat cooled down and everyone in the camp started to bustle about and gathered around, they heard the Buddha teaching. They heard his voice, and it was also perfected, was of perfect calmness, was full of peace. Gotama taught the teachings of suffering, of the origin of suffering, of the way to relieve suffering. Calmly and clearly his quiet speech flowed on. Suffering was life, full of suffering was the world, but salvation from suffering had been found: salvation was obtained by him who would walk the path of the Buddha. With a soft, yet firm voice the exalted one spoke, taught the four main doctrines, taught the eightfold path, patiently he went the usual path of the teachings, of the examples, of the repetitions, brightly and quietly his voice hovered over the listeners, like a light, like a starry sky.

When the Buddha—night had already fallen—ended his speech, many a pilgrim stepped forward and asked to accepted into the community, sought refuge in the teachings. And Gotama accepted them by speaking: "You have heard the teachings well, it has come to you well. Thus join us and walk in holiness, to put an end to all suffering."

Behold, then Govinda, the shy one, also stepped forward and spoke: "I also take my refuge in the exalted one and his teachings," and he asked to accepted into the community of his disciples and was accepted.

Right afterwards, when the Buddha had retired for the night, Govinda turned to Siddhartha and spoke eagerly: "Siddhartha, it is not my place to scold you. We have both heard the exalted one, we have both perceived the teachings. Govinda has heard the teachings, he has taken refuge in it. But you, my honoured friend, don't you also want to walk the path of salvation? Would you want to hesitate, do you want to wait any longer?"

Siddhartha awakened as if he had been asleep, when he heard Govinda's words. For a long tome, he looked into Govinda's face. Then he spoke quietly, in a voice without mockery: "Govinda, my friend, now you have taken this step, now you have chosen this path. Always, oh Govinda, you've been my friend, you've always walked one step behind me. Often I have thought: Won't Govinda for once also take a step by himself, without me, out of his own soul? Behold, now you've turned into a man and are choosing your path for yourself. I wish that you would go it up to its end, oh my friend, that you shall find salvation!"

Govinda, not completely understanding it yet, repeated his question in an impatient tone: "Speak up, I beg you, my dear! Tell me, since it could not be any other way, that you also, my learned friend, will take your refuge with the exalted Buddha!"

Siddhartha placed his hand on Govinda's shoulder: "You failed to hear my good wish for you, oh Govinda. I'm repeating it: I wish that you would go this path up to its end, that you shall find salvation!"

In this moment, Govinda realized that his friend had left him, and he started to weep.

"Siddhartha!" he exclaimed lamentingly.

Siddhartha kindly spoke to him: "Don't forget, Govinda, that you are now one of the Samanas of the Buddha! You have renounced your home and your parents, renounced your birth and possessions, renounced your free will, renounced all friendship. This is what the teachings require, this is what the exalted one wants. This is what you wanted for yourself. Tomorrow, oh Govinda, I'll leave you."

For a long time, the friends continued walking in the grove; for a long time, they lay there and found no sleep. And over and over again, Govinda urged his friend, he should tell him why he would not want to seek refuge in Gotama's teachings, what fault he would find in these teachings. But Siddhartha turned him away every time and said: "Be content, Govinda! Very good are the teachings of the exalted one, how could I find a fault in them?"

Very early in the morning, a follower of Buddha, one of his oldest monks, went through the garden and called all those to him who had as novices taken their refuge in the teachings, to dress them up in the yellow robe and to instruct them in the first teachings and duties of their position. Then Govinda broke loose, embraced once again his childhood friend and left with the novices.

But Siddhartha walked through the grove, lost in thought.

Then he happened to meet Gotama, the exalted one, and when he greeted him with respect and the Buddha's glance was so full of kindness and calm, the young man summoned his courage and asked the venerable one for the permission to talk to him. Silently the exalted one nodded his approval.

Quoth Siddhartha: "Yesterday, oh exalted one, I had been privileged to hear your wondrous teachings. Together with my friend, I had come from afar, to hear your teachings. And now my friend is going to stay with your people, he has taken his refuge with you. But I will again start on my pilgrimage."

"As you please," the venerable one spoke politely.

"Too bold is my speech," Siddhartha continued, "but I do not want to leave the exalted one without having honestly told him my thoughts. Does it please the venerable one to listen to me for one moment longer?"

Silently, the Buddha nodded his approval.

Quoth Siddhartha: "One thing, oh most venerable one, I have admired in your teachings most of all. Everything in your teachings is perfectly clear, is proven; you are presenting the world as a perfect chain, a chain which is never and nowhere broken, an eternal chain the links of which are causes and effects. Never before, this has been seen so clearly; never before, this has been presented so irrefutably; truly, the heart of every Brahman has to beat stronger with love, once he has seen the world through your teachings perfectly connected, without gaps, clear as a crystal, not depending on chance, not depending on gods. Whether it may be good or bad, whether living according to it would be suffering or joy, I do not wish to discuss, possibly this is not essential—but the uniformity of the world, that everything which happens is connected, that the great and the small things are all encompassed by the same forces of time, by the same law of causes, of coming into being and of dying, this is what shines brightly out of your exalted teachings, oh perfected one. But according to your very own teachings, this unity and necessary sequence of all things is nevertheless broken in one place, through a small gap, this world of unity is invaded by something alien, something new, something which had not been there before, and which cannot be demonstrated and cannot be proven: these are your teachings of overcoming the world, of salvation. But with this small gap, with this small breach, the entire eternal and uniform law of the world is breaking apart again and becomes void. Please forgive me for expressing this objection."

Quietly, Gotama had listened to him, unmoved. Now he spoke, the perfected one, with his kind, with his polite and clear voice: "You've heard the teachings, oh son of a Brahman, and good for you that you've thought about it thus deeply. You've found a gap in it, an error. You should think about this further. But be warned, oh seeker of knowledge, of the thicket of opinions and of arguing about words. There is nothing to opinions, they may be beautiful or ugly, smart or foolish, everyone can support them or discard them. But the teachings, you've heard from me, are no opinion, and their goal is not to explain the world to those who seek knowledge. They have a different goal; their goal is salvation from suffering. This is what Gotama teaches, nothing else."

"I wish that you, oh exalted one, would not be angry with me," said the young man. "I have not spoken to you like this to argue with you, to argue about words. You are truly right, there is little to opinions. But let me say this one more thing: I have not doubted in you for a single moment. I have not doubted for a single moment that you are Buddha, that you have reached the goal, the highest goal towards which so many thousands of Brahmans and sons of Brahmans are on their way. You have found salvation from death. It has come to you in the course of your own search, on your own path, through thoughts, through meditation, through realizations, through enlightenment. It has not come to you by means of teachings! And—thus is my thought, oh exalted one,—nobody will obtain salvation by means of teachings! You will not be able to convey and say to anybody, oh venerable one, in words and through teachings what has happened to you in the hour of enlightenment! The teachings of the enlightened Buddha contain much, it teaches many to live righteously, to avoid evil. But there is one thing which these so clear, these so venerable teachings do not contain: they do not contain the mystery of what the exalted one has experienced for himself, he alone among hundreds of thousands. This is what I have thought and realized, when I have heard the teachings. This is why I am continuing my travels—not to seek other, better teachings, for I know there are none, but to depart from all teachings and all teachers and to reach my goal by myself or to die. But often, I'll think of this day, oh exalted one, and of this hour, when my eyes beheld a holy man."

The Buddha's eyes quietly looked to the ground; quietly, in perfect equanimity his inscrutable face was smiling.

"I wish," the venerable one spoke slowly, "that your thoughts shall not be in error, that you shall reach the goal! But tell me: Have you seen the multitude of my Samanas, my many brothers, who have taken refuge in the teachings? And do you believe, oh stranger, oh Samana, do you believe that it would be better for them all the abandon the teachings and to return into the life the world and of desires?"

"Far is such a thought from my mind," exclaimed Siddhartha. "I wish that they shall all stay with the teachings, that they shall reach their goal! It is not my place to judge another person's life. Only for myself, for myself alone, I must decide, I must chose, I must refuse. Salvation from the self is what we Samanas search for, oh exalted one. If I merely were one of your disciples, oh venerable one, I'd fear that it might happen to me that only seemingly, only deceptively my self would be calm and be redeemed, but that in truth it would live on and grow, for then I had replaced my self with the teachings, my duty to follow you, my love for you, and the community of the monks!"

With half of a smile, with an unwavering openness and kindness, Gotama looked into the stranger's eyes and bid him to leave with a hardly noticeable gesture.

"You are wise, oh Samana.", the venerable one spoke.

"You know how to talk wisely, my friend. Be aware of too much wisdom!"

The Buddha turned away, and his glance and half of a smile remained forever etched in Siddhartha's memory.

I have never before seen a person glance and smile, sit and walk this way, he thought; truly, I wish to be able to glance and smile, sit and walk this way, too, thus free, thus venerable, thus concealed, thus open, thus child-like and mysterious. Truly, only a person who has succeeded in reaching the innermost part of his self would glance and walk this way. Well so, I also will seek to reach the innermost part of my self.

I saw a man, Siddhartha thought, a single man, before whom I would have to lower my glance. I do not want to lower my glance before any other, not before any other. No teachings will entice me any more, since this man's teachings have not enticed me.

I am deprived by the Buddha, thought Siddhartha, I am deprived, and even more he has given to me. He has deprived me of my friend, the one who had believed in me and now believes in him, who had been my shadow and is now Gotama's shadow. But he has given me Siddhartha, myself.

## AWAKENING

When Siddhartha left the grove, where the Buddha, the perfected one, stayed behind, where Govinda stayed behind, then he felt that in this grove his past life also stayed behind and parted from him. He pondered about this sensation, which filled him completely, as he was slowly walking along. He pondered deeply, like diving into a deep water he let himself sink down to the ground of the sensation, down to the place where the causes lie, because to identify the causes, so it seemed to him, is the very essence of thinking, and by this alone sensations turn into realizations and are not lost, but become entities and start to emit like rays of light what is inside of them.

Slowly walking along, Siddhartha pondered. He realized that he was no youth any more, but had turned into a man. He realized that one thing had left him, as a snake is left by its old skin, that one thing no longer existed in him, which had accompanied him throughout his youth and used to be a part of him: the wish to have teachers and to listen to teachings. He had also left the last teacher who had appeared on his path, even him, the highest and wisest teacher, the most holy one, Buddha, he had left him, had to part with him, was not able to accept his teachings.

Slower, he walked along in his thoughts and asked himself: "But what is this, what you have sought to learn from teachings and from teachers, and what they, who have taught you much, were still unable to teach you?" And he found: "It was the self, the purpose and essence of which I sought to learn. It was the self, I wanted to free myself from, which I sought to overcome. But I was not able to overcome it, could only deceive it, could only flee from it, only hide from it. Truly, no thing in this world has kept my thoughts thus busy, as this my very own self, this mystery of me being alive, of me being one and being separated and isolated from all others, of me being Siddhartha! And there is no thing in this world I know less about than about me, about Siddhartha!"

Having been pondering while slowly walking along, he now stopped as these thoughts caught hold of him, and right away another thought sprang forth from these, a new thought, which was: "That I know nothing about myself, that Siddhartha has remained thus alien and unknown to me, stems from one cause, a single cause: I was afraid of myself, I was fleeing from myself! I searched Atman, I searched Brahman, I was willing to to dissect my self and peel off all of its layers, to find the core of all peels in its unknown interior, the Atman, life, the divine part, the ultimate part. But I have lost myself in the process."

Siddhartha opened his eyes and looked around, a smile filled his face and a feeling of awakening from long dreams flowed through him from his head down to his toes. And it was not long before he walked again, walked quickly like a man who knows what he has got to do.

"Oh," he thought, taking a deep breath, "now I would not let Siddhartha escape from me again! No longer, I want to begin my thoughts and my life with Atman and with the suffering of the world. I do not want to kill and dissect myself any longer, to find a secret behind the ruins. Neither Yoga-Veda shall teach me any more, nor Atharva-Veda, nor the ascetics, nor any kind of teachings. I want to learn from myself, want to be my student, want to get to know myself, the secret of Siddhartha."

He looked around, as if he was seeing the world for the first time. Beautiful was the world, colourful was the world, strange and mysterious was the world! Here was blue, here was yellow, here was green, the sky and the river flowed, the forest and the mountains were rigid, all of it was beautiful, all of it was mysterious and magical, and in its midst was he, Siddhartha, the awakening one, on the path to himself. All of this, all this yellow and blue, river and forest, entered Siddhartha for the first time through the eyes, was no longer a spell of Mara, was no longer the veil of Maya, was no longer a pointless and coincidental diversity of mere appearances, despicable to the deeply thinking Brahman, who scorns diversity, who seeks unity. Blue was blue, river was river, and if also in the blue and the river, in Siddhartha, the singular and divine lived hidden, so it was still that very divinity's way and purpose, to be here yellow, here blue, there sky, there forest, and here Siddhartha. The purpose and the essential properties were not somewhere behind the things, they were in them, in everything.

"How deaf and stupid have I been!" he thought, walking swiftly along. "When someone reads a text, wants to discover its meaning, he will not scorn the symbols and letters and call them deceptions, coincidence, and worthless hull, but he will read them, he will study and love them, letter by letter. But I, who wanted to read the book of the world and the book of my own being, I have, for the sake of a meaning I had anticipated before I read, scorned the symbols and letters, I called the visible world a deception, called my eyes and my tongue coincidental and worthless forms without substance. No, this is over, I have awakened, I have indeed awakened and have not been born before this very day."

In thinking this thoughts, Siddhartha stopped once again, suddenly, as if there was a snake lying in front of him on the path.

Because suddenly, he had also become aware of this: He, who was indeed like someone who had just woken up or like a new-born baby, he had to start his life anew and start again at the very beginning. When he had left in this very morning from the grove Jetavana, the grove of that exalted one, already awakening, already on the path towards himself, he he had every intention, regarded as natural and took for granted, that he, after years as an ascetic, would return to his home and his father. But now, only in this moment, when he stopped as if a snake was lying on his path, he also awoke to this realization: "But I am no longer the one I was, I am no ascetic any more, I am not a priest any more, I am no Brahman any more. Whatever should I do at home and at my father's place? Study? Make offerings? Practise meditation? But all this is over, all of this is no longer alongside my path."

Motionless, Siddhartha remained standing there, and for the time of one moment and breath, his heart felt cold, he felt a cold in his chest, as a small animal, a bird or a rabbit, would when seeing how alone he was. For many years, he had been without home and had felt nothing. Now, he felt it. Still, even in the deepest meditation, he had been his father's son, had been a Brahman, of a high caste, a cleric. Now, he was nothing but Siddhartha, the awoken one, nothing else was left. Deeply, he inhaled, and for a moment, he felt cold and shivered. Nobody was thus alone as he was. There was no nobleman who did not belong to the noblemen, no worker that did not belong to the workers, and found refuge with them, shared their life, spoke their language. No Brahman, who would not be regarded as Brahmans and lived with them, no ascetic who would not find his refuge in the caste of the Samanas, and even the most forlorn hermit in the forest was not just one and alone, he was also surrounded by a place he belonged to, he also belonged to a caste, in which he was at home. Govinda had become a monk, and a thousand monks were his brothers, wore the same robe as he, believed in his faith, spoke his language. But he, Siddhartha, where did he belong to? With whom would he share his life? Whose language would he speak?

Out of this moment, when the world melted away all around him, when he stood alone like a star in the sky, out of this moment of a cold and despair, Siddhartha emerged, more a self than before, more firmly concentrated. He felt: This had been the last tremor of the awakening, the last struggle of this birth. And it was not long until he walked again in long strides, started to proceed swiftly and impatiently, heading no longer for home, no longer to his father, no longer back.

# SECOND PART

## Dedicated to Wilhelm Gundert, my cousin in Japan

# KAMALA

Siddhartha learned something new on every step of his path, for the world was transformed, and his heart was enchanted. He saw the sun rising over the mountains with their forests and setting over the distant beach with its palm-trees. At night, he saw the stars in the sky in their fixed positions and the crescent of the moon floating like a boat in the blue. He saw trees, stars, animals, clouds, rainbows, rocks, herbs, flowers, stream and river, the glistening dew in the bushes in the morning, distant hight mountains which were blue and pale, birds sang and bees, wind silverishly blew through the rice-field. All of this, a thousand-fold and colourful, had always been there, always the sun and the moon had shone, always rivers had roared and bees had buzzed, but in former times all of this had been nothing more to Siddhartha than a fleeting, deceptive veil before his eyes, looked upon in distrust, destined to be penetrated and destroyed by thought, since it was not the essential existence, since this essence lay beyond, on the other side of, the visible. But now, his liberated eyes stayed on this side, he saw and became aware of the visible, sought to be at home in this world, did not search for the true essence, did not aim at a world beyond. Beautiful was this world, looking at it thus, without searching, thus simply, thus childlike. Beautiful were the moon and the stars, beautiful was the stream and the banks, the forest and the rocks, the goat and the gold-beetle, the flower and the butterfly. Beautiful and lovely it was, thus to walk through the world, thus childlike, thus awoken, thus open to what is near, thus without distrust. Differently the sun burnt the head, differently the shade of the forest cooled him down, differently the stream and the cistern, the pumpkin and the banana tasted. Short were the days, short the nights, every hour sped swiftly away like a sail on the sea, and under the sail was a ship full of treasures, full of joy. Siddhartha saw a group of apes moving through the high canopy of the forest, high in the branches, and heard their savage, greedy song. Siddhartha saw a male sheep following a female one and mating with her. In a lake of reeds, he saw the pike hungrily hunting for its dinner; propelling themselves away from it, in fear, wiggling and sparkling, the young fish jumped in droves out of the water; the scent of strength and passion came forcefully out of the hasty eddies of the water, which the pike stirred up, impetuously hunting.

All of this had always existed, and he had not seen it; he had not been with it. Now he was with it, he was part of it. Light and shadow ran through his eyes, stars and moon ran through his heart.

On the way, Siddhartha also remembered everything he had experienced in the Garden Jetavana, the teaching he had heard there, the divine Buddha, the farewell from Govinda, the conversation with the exalted one. Again he remembered his own words, he had spoken to the exalted one, every word, and with astonishment he became aware of the fact that there he had said things which he had not really known yet at this time. What he had said to Gotama: his, the Buddha's, treasure and secret was not the teachings, but the unexpressable and not teachable, which he had experienced in the hour of his enlightenment—it was nothing but this very thing which he had now gone to experience, what he now began to experience. Now, he had to experience his self. It is true that he had already known for a long time that his self was Atman, in its essence bearing the same eternal characteristics as Brahman. But never, he had really found this self, because he had wanted to capture it in the net of thought. With the body definitely not being the self, and not the spectacle of the senses, so it also was not the thought, not the rational mind, not the learned wisdom, not the learned ability to draw conclusions and to develop previous thoughts in to new ones. No, this world of thought was also still on this side, and nothing could be achieved by killing the random self of the senses, if the random self of thoughts and learned knowledge was fattened on the other hand. Both, the thoughts as well as the senses, were pretty things, the ultimate meaning was hidden behind both of them, both had to be listened to, both had to be played with, both neither had to be scorned nor overestimated, from both the secret voices of the innermost truth had to be attentively perceived. He wanted to strive for nothing, except for what the voice commanded him to strive for, dwell on nothing, except where the voice would advise him to do so. Why had Gotama, at that time, in the hour of all hours, sat down under the bo-tree, where the enlightenment hit him? He had heard a voice, a voice in his own heart, which had commanded him to seek rest under this tree, and he had neither preferred self-castigation, offerings, ablutions, nor prayer, neither food nor drink, neither sleep nor dream, he had obeyed the voice. To obey like this, not to an external command, only to the voice, to be ready like this, this was good, this was necessary, nothing else was necessary.

In the night when he slept in the straw hut of a ferryman by the river, Siddhartha had a dream: Govinda was standing in front of him, dressed in the yellow robe of an ascetic. Sad was how Govinda looked like, sadly he asked: Why have you forsaken me? At this, he embraced Govinda, wrapped his arms around him, and as he was pulling him close to his chest and kissed him, it was not Govinda any more, but a woman, and a full breast popped out of the woman's dress, at which Siddhartha lay and drank, sweetly and strongly tasted the milk from this breast. It tasted of woman and man, of sun and forest, of animal and flower, of every fruit, of every joyful desire. It intoxicated him and rendered him unconscious.—When Siddhartha woke up, the pale river shimmered through the door of the hut, and in the forest, a dark call of an owl resounded deeply and pleasantly.

When the day began, Siddhartha asked his host, the ferryman, to get him across the river. The ferryman got him across the river on his bamboo-raft, the wide water shimmered reddishly in the light of the morning.

"This is a beautiful river," he said to his companion.

"Yes," said the ferryman, "a very beautiful river, I love it more than anything. Often I have listened to it, often I have looked into its eyes, and always I have learned from it. Much can be learned from a river."

"I than you, my benefactor," spoke Siddhartha, disembarking on the other side of the river. "I have no gift I could give you for your hospitality, my dear, and also no payment for your work. I am a man without a home, a son of a Brahman and a Samana."

"I did see it," spoke the ferryman, "and I haven't expected any payment from you and no gift which would be the custom for guests to bear. You will give me the gift another time."

"Do you think so?" asked Siddhartha amusedly.

"Surely. This too, I have learned from the river: everything is coming back! You too, Samana, will come back. Now farewell! Let your friendship be my reward. Commemorate me, when you'll make offerings to the gods."

Smiling, they parted. Smiling, Siddhartha was happy about the friendship and the kindness of the ferryman. "He is like Govinda," he thought with a smile, "all I meet on my path are like Govinda. All are thankful, though they are the ones who would have a right to receive thanks. All are submissive, all would like to be friends, like to obey, think little. Like children are all people."

At about noon, he came through a village. In front of the mud cottages, children were rolling about in the street, were playing with pumpkin-seeds and sea-shells, screamed and wrestled, but they all timidly fled from the unknown Samana. In the end of the village, the path led through a stream, and by the side of the stream, a young woman was kneeling and washing clothes. When Siddhartha greeted her, she lifted her head and looked up to him with a smile, so that he saw the white in her eyes glistening. He called out a blessing to her, as it is the custom among travellers, and asked how far he still had to go to reach the large city. Then she got up and came to him, beautifully her wet mouth was shimmering in her young face. She exchanged humorous banter with him, asked whether he had eaten already, and whether it was true that the Samanas slept alone in the forest at night and were not allowed to have any women with them. While talking, she put her left foot on his right one and made a movement as a woman does who would want to initiate that kind of sexual pleasure with a man, which the textbooks call "climbing a tree". Siddhartha felt his blood heating up, and since in this moment he had to think of his dream again, he bend slightly down to the woman and kissed with his lips the brown nipple of her breast. Looking up, he saw her face smiling full of lust and her eyes, with contracted pupils, begging with desire.

Siddhartha also felt desire and felt the source of his sexuality moving; but since he had never touched a woman before, he hesitated for a moment, while his hands were already prepared to reach out for her. And in this moment he heard, shuddering with awe, the voice if his innermost self, and this voice said No. Then, all charms disappeared from the young woman's smiling face, he no longer saw anything else but the damp glance of a female animal in heat. Politely, he petted her cheek, turned away from her and disappeared away from the disappointed woman with light steps into the bamboo-wood.

On this day, he reached the large city before the evening, and was happy, for he felt the need to be among people. For a long time, he had lived in the forests, and the straw hut of the ferryman, in which he had slept that night, had been the first roof for a long time he has had over his head.

Before the city, in a beautifully fenced grove, the traveller came across a small group of servants, both male and female, carrying baskets. In their midst, carried by four servants in an ornamental sedan-chair, sat a woman, the mistress, on red pillows under a colourful canopy. Siddhartha stopped at the entrance to the pleasure-garden and watched the parade, saw the servants, the maids, the baskets, saw the sedan-chair and saw the lady in it. Under black hair, which made to tower high on her head, he saw a very fair, very delicate, very smart face, a brightly red mouth, like a freshly cracked fig, eyebrows which were well tended and painted in a high arch, smart and watchful dark eyes, a clear, tall neck rising from a green and golden garment, resting fair hands, long and thin, with wide golden bracelets over the wrists.

Siddhartha saw how beautiful she was, and his heart rejoiced. He bowed deeply, when the sedan-chair came closer, and straightening up again, he looked at the fair, charming face, read for a moment in the smart eyes with the high arcs above, breathed in a slight fragrant, he did not know. With a smile, the beautiful women nodded for a moment and disappeared into the grove, and then the servant as well.

Thus I am entering this city, Siddhartha thought, with a charming omen. He instantly felt drawn into the grove, but he thought about it, and only now he became aware of how the servants and maids had looked at him at the entrance, how despicable, how distrustful, how rejecting.

I am still a Samana, he thought, I am still an ascetic and beggar. I must not remain like this, I will not be able to enter the grove like this. And he laughed.

The next person who came along this path he asked about the grove and for the name of the woman, and was told that this was the grove of Kamala, the famous courtesan, and that, aside from the grove, she owned a house in the city.

Then, he entered the city. Now he had a goal.

Pursuing his goal, he allowed the city to suck him in, drifted through the flow of the streets, stood still on the squares, rested on the stairs of stone by the river. When the evening came, he made friends with barber's assistant, whom he had seen working in the shade of an arch in a building, whom he found again praying in a temple of Vishnu, whom he told about stories of Vishnu and the Lakshmi. Among the boats by the river, he slept this night, and early in the morning, before the first customers came into his shop, he had the barber's assistant shave his beard and cut his hair, comb his hair and anoint it with fine oil. Then he went to take his bath in the river.

When late in the afternoon, beautiful Kamala approached her grove in her sedan-chair, Siddhartha was standing at the entrance, made a bow and received the courtesan's greeting. But that servant who walked at the very end of her train he motioned to him and asked him to inform his mistress that a young Brahman would wish to talk to her. After a while, the servant returned, asked him, who had been waiting, to follow him conducted him, who was following him, without a word into a pavilion, where Kamala was lying on a couch, and left him alone with her.

"Weren't you already standing out there yesterday, greeting me?" asked Kamala.

"It's true that I've already seen and greeted you yesterday."

"But didn't you yesterday wear a beard, and long hair, and dust in your hair?"

"You have observed well, you have seen everything. You have seen Siddhartha, the son of a Brahman, who has left his home to become a Samana, and who has been a Samana for three years. But now, I have left that path and came into this city, and the first one I met, even before I had entered the city, was you. To say this, I have come to you, oh Kamala! You are the first woman whom Siddhartha is not addressing with his eyes turned to the ground. Never again I want to turn my eyes to the ground, when I'm coming across a beautiful woman."

Kamala smiled and played with her fan of peacocks' feathers. And asked: "And only to tell me this, Siddhartha has come to me?"

"To tell you this and to thank you for being so beautiful. And if it doesn't displease you, Kamala, I would like to ask you to be my friend and teacher, for I know nothing yet of that art which you have mastered in the highest degree."

At this, Kamala laughed aloud.

"Never before this has happened to me, my friend, that a Samana from the forest came to me and wanted to learn from me! Never before this has happened to me, that a Samana came to me with long hair and an old, torn loin-cloth! Many young men come to me, and there are also sons of Brahmans among them, but they come in beautiful clothes, they come in fine shoes, they have perfume in their hair and money in their pouches. This is, oh Samana, how the young men are like who come to me."

Quoth Siddhartha: "Already I am starting to learn from you. Even yesterday, I was already learning. I have already taken off my beard, have combed the hair, have oil in my hair. There is little which is still missing in me, oh excellent one: fine clothes, fine shoes, money in my pouch. You shall know, Siddhartha has set harder goals for himself than such trifles, and he has reached them. How shouldn't I reach that goal, which I have set for myself yesterday: to be your friend and to learn the joys of love from you! You'll see that I'll learn quickly, Kamala, I have already learned harder things than what you're supposed to teach me. And now let's get to it: You aren't satisfied with Siddhartha as he is, with oil in his hair, but without clothes, without shoes, without money?"

Laughing, Kamala exclaimed: "No, my dear, he doesn't satisfy me yet. Clothes are what he must have, pretty clothes, and shoes, pretty shoes, and lots of money in his pouch, and gifts for Kamala. Do you know it now, Samana from the forest? Did you mark my words?"

"Yes, I have marked your words," Siddhartha exclaimed. "How should I not mark words which are coming from such a mouth! Your mouth is like a freshly cracked fig, Kamala. My mouth is red and fresh as well, it will be a suitable match for yours, you'll see.—But tell me, beautiful Kamala, aren't you at all afraid of the Samana from the forest, who has come to learn how to make love?"

"Whatever for should I be afraid of a Samana, a stupid Samana from the forest, who is coming from the jackals and doesn't even know yet what women are?"

"Oh, he's strong, the Samana, and he isn't afraid of anything. He could force you, beautiful girl. He could kidnap you. He could hurt you."

"No, Samana, I am not afraid of this. Did any Samana or Brahman ever fear, someone might come and grab him and steal his learning, and his religious devotion, and his depth of thought? No, for they are his very own, and he would only give away from those whatever he is willing to give and to whomever he is willing to give. Like this it is, precisely like this it is also with Kamala and with the pleasures of love. Beautiful and red is Kamala's mouth, but just try to kiss it against Kamala's will, and you will not obtain a single drop of sweetness from it, which knows how to give so many sweet things! You are learning easily, Siddhartha, thus you should also learn this: love can be obtained by begging, buying, receiving it as a gift, finding it in the street, but it cannot be stolen. In this, you have come up with the wrong path. No, it would be a pity, if a pretty young man like you would want to tackle it in such a wrong manner."

Siddhartha bowed with a smile. "It would be a pity, Kamala, you are so right! It would be such a great pity. No, I shall not lose a single drop of sweetness from your mouth, nor you from mine! So it is settled: Siddhartha will return, once he'll have have what he still lacks: clothes, shoes, money. But speak, lovely Kamala, couldn't you still give me one small advice?"

"An advice? Why not? Who wouldn't like to give an advice to a poor, ignorant Samana, who is coming from the jackals of the forest?"

"Dear Kamala, thus advise me where I should go to, that I'll find these three things most quickly?"

"Friend, many would like to know this. You must do what you've learned and ask for money, clothes, and shoes in return. There is no other way for a poor man to obtain money. What might you be able to do?"

"I can think. I can wait. I can fast."

"Nothing else?"

"Nothing. But yes, I can also write poetry. Would you like to give me a kiss for a poem?"

"I would like to, if I'll like your poem. What would be its title?"

Siddhartha spoke, after he had thought about it for a moment, these verses:

Into her shady grove stepped the pretty Kamala, At the grove's entrance stood the brown Samana. Deeply, seeing the lotus's blossom, Bowed that man, and smiling Kamala thanked. More lovely, thought the young man, than offerings for gods, More lovely is offering to pretty Kamala.

Kamala loudly clapped her hands, so that the golden bracelets clanged.

"Beautiful are your verses, oh brown Samana, and truly, I'm losing nothing when I'm giving you a kiss for them."

She beckoned him with her eyes, he tilted his head so that his face touched hers and placed his mouth on that mouth which was like a freshly cracked fig. For a long time, Kamala kissed him, and with a deep astonishment Siddhartha felt how she taught him, how wise she was, how she controlled him, rejected him, lured him, and how after this first one there was to be a long, a well ordered, well tested sequence of kisses, everyone different from the others, he was still to receive. Breathing deeply, he remained standing where he was, and was in this moment astonished like a child about the cornucopia of knowledge and things worth learning, which revealed itself before his eyes.

"Very beautiful are your verses," exclaimed Kamala, "if I was rich, I would give you pieces of gold for them. But it will be difficult for you to earn thus much money with verses as you need. For you need a lot of money, if you want to be Kamala's friend."

"The way you're able to kiss, Kamala!" stammered Siddhartha.

"Yes, this I am able to do, therefore I do not lack clothes, shoes, bracelets, and all beautiful things. But what will become of you? Aren't you able to do anything else but thinking, fasting, making poetry?"

"I also know the sacrificial songs," said Siddhartha, "but I do not want to sing them any more. I also know magic spells, but I do not want to speak them any more. I have read the scriptures—"

"Stop," Kamala interrupted him. "You're able to read? And write?"

"Certainly, I can do this. Many people can do this."

"Most people can't. I also can't do it. It is very good that you're able to read and write, very good. You will also still find use for the magic spells."

In this moment, a maid came running in and whispered a message into her mistress's ear.

"There's a visitor for me," exclaimed Kamala. "Hurry and get yourself away, Siddhartha, nobody may see you in here, remember this! Tomorrow, I'll see you again."

But to the maid she gave the order to give the pious Brahman white upper garments. Without fully understanding what was happening to him, Siddhartha found himself being dragged away by the maid, brought into a garden-house avoiding the direct path, being given upper garments as a gift, led into the bushes, and urgently admonished to get himself out of the grove as soon as possible without being seen.

Contently, he did as he had been told. Being accustomed to the forest, he managed to get out of the grove and over the hedge without making a sound. Contently, he returned to the city, carrying the rolled up garments under his arm. At the inn, where travellers stay, he positioned himself by the door, without words he asked for food, without a word he accepted a piece of rice-cake. Perhaps as soon as tomorrow, he thought, I will ask no one for food any more.

Suddenly, pride flared up in him. He was no Samana any more, it was no longer becoming to him to beg. He gave the rice-cake to a dog and remained without food.

"Simple is the life which people lead in this world here," thought Siddhartha. "It presents no difficulties. Everything was difficult, toilsome, and ultimately hopeless, when I was still a Samana. Now, everything is easy, easy like that lessons in kissing, which Kamala is giving me. I need clothes and money, nothing else; this a small, near goals, they won't make a person lose any sleep."

He had already discovered Kamala's house in the city long before, there he turned up the following day.

"Things are working out well," she called out to him. "They are expecting you at Kamaswami's, he is the richest merchant of the city. If he'll like you, he'll accept you into his service. Be smart, brown Samana. I had others tell him about you. Be polite towards him, he is very powerful. But don't be too modest! I do not want you to become his servant, you shall become his equal, or else I won't be satisfied with you. Kamaswami is starting to get old and lazy. If he'll like you, he'll entrust you with a lot."

Siddhartha thanked her and laughed, and when she found out that he had not eaten anything yesterday and today, she sent for bread and fruits and treated him to it.

"You've been lucky," she said when they parted, "I'm opening one door after another for you. How come? Do you have a spell?"

Siddhartha said: "Yesterday, I told you I knew how to think, to wait, and to fast, but you thought this was of no use. But it is useful for many things, Kamala, you'll see. You'll see that the stupid Samanas are learning and able to do many pretty things in the forest, which the likes of you aren't capable of. The day before yesterday, I was still a shaggy beggar, as soon as yesterday I have kissed Kamala, and soon I'll be a merchant and have money and all those things you insist upon."

"Well yes," she admitted. "But where would you be without me? What would you be, if Kamala wasn't helping you?"

"Dear Kamala," said Siddhartha and straightened up to his full height, "when I came to you into your grove, I did the first step. It was my resolution to learn love from this most beautiful woman. From that moment on when I had made this resolution, I also knew that I would carry it out. I knew that you would help me, at your first glance at the entrance of the grove I already knew it."

"But what if I hadn't been willing?"

"You were willing. Look, Kamala: When you throw a rock into the water, it will speed on the fastest course to the bottom of the water. This is how it is when Siddhartha has a goal, a resolution. Siddhartha does nothing, he waits, he thinks, he fasts, but he passes through the things of the world like a rock through water, without doing anything, without stirring; he is drawn, he lets himself fall. His goal attracts him, because he doesn't let anything enter his soul which might oppose the goal. This is what Siddhartha has learned among the Samanas. This is what fools call magic and of which they think it would be effected by means of the daemons. Nothing is effected by daemons, there are no daemons. Everyone can perform magic, everyone can reach his goals, if he is able to think, if he is able to wait, if he is able to fast."

Kamala listened to him. She loved his voice, she loved the look from his eyes.

"Perhaps it is so," she said quietly, "as you say, friend. But perhaps it is also like this: that Siddhartha is a handsome man, that his glance pleases the women, that therefore good fortune is coming towards him."

With one kiss, Siddhartha bid his farewell. "I wish that it should be this way, my teacher; that my glance shall please you, that always good fortune shall come to me out of your direction!"

## WITH THE CHILDLIKE PEOPLE

Siddhartha went to Kamaswami the merchant, he was directed into a rich house, servants led him between precious carpets into a chamber, where he awaited the master of the house.

Kamaswami entered, a swiftly, smoothly moving man with very gray hair, with very intelligent, cautious eyes, with a greedy mouth. Politely, the host and the guest greeted one another.

"I have been told," the merchant began, "that you were a Brahman, a learned man, but that you seek to be in the service of a merchant. Might you have become destitute, Brahman, so that you seek to serve?"

"No," said Siddhartha, "I have not become destitute and have never been destitute. You should know that I'm coming from the Samanas, with whom I have lived for a long time."

"If you're coming from the Samanas, how could you be anything but destitute? Aren't the Samanas entirely without possessions?"

"I am without possessions," said Siddhartha, "if this is what you mean. Surely, I am without possessions. But I am so voluntarily, and therefore I am not destitute."

"But what are you planning to live of, being without possessions?"

"I haven't thought of this yet, sir. For more than three years, I have been without possessions, and have never thought about of what I should live."

"So you've lived of the possessions of others."

"Presumable this is how it is. After all, a merchant also lives of what other people own."

"Well said. But he wouldn't take anything from another person for nothing; he would give his merchandise in return."

"So it seems to be indeed. Everyone takes, everyone gives, such is life."

"But if you don't mind me asking: being without possessions, what would you like to give?"

"Everyone gives what he has. The warrior gives strength, the merchant gives merchandise, the teacher teachings, the farmer rice, the fisher fish."

"Yes indeed. And what is it now what you've got to give? What is it that you've learned, what you're able to do?"

"I can think. I can wait. I can fast."

"That's everything?"

"I believe, that's everything!"

"And what's the use of that? For example, the fasting—what is it good for?"

"It is very good, sir. When a person has nothing to eat, fasting is the smartest thing he could do. When, for example, Siddhartha hadn't learned to fast, he would have to accept any kind of service before this day is up, whether it may be with you or wherever, because hunger would force him to do so. But like this, Siddhartha can wait calmly, he knows no impatience, he knows no emergency, for a long time he can allow hunger to besiege him and can laugh about it. This, sir, is what fasting is good for."

"You're right, Samana. Wait for a moment."

Kamaswami left the room and returned with a scroll, which he handed to his guest while asking: "Can you read this?"

Siddhartha looked at the scroll, on which a sales-contract had been written down, and began to read out its contents.

"Excellent," said Kamaswami. "And would you write something for me on this piece of paper?"

He handed him a piece of paper and a pen, and Siddhartha wrote and returned the paper.

Kamaswami read: "Writing is good, thinking is better. Being smart is good, being patient is better."

"It is excellent how you're able to write," the merchant praised him. "Many a thing we will still have to discuss with one another. For today, I'm asking you to be my guest and to live in this house."

Siddhartha thanked and accepted, and lived in the dealers house from now on. Clothes were brought to him, and shoes, and every day, a servant prepared a bath for him. Twice a day, a plentiful meal was served, but Siddhartha only ate once a day, and ate neither meat nor did he drink wine. Kamaswami told him about his trade, showed him the merchandise and storage-rooms, showed him calculations. Siddhartha got to know many new things, he heard a lot and spoke little. And thinking of Kamala's words, he was never subservient to the merchant, forced him to treat him as an equal, yes even more than an equal. Kamaswami conducted his business with care and often with passion, but Siddhartha looked upon all of this as if it was a game, the rules of which he tried hard to learn precisely, but the contents of which did not touch his heart.

He was not in Kamaswami's house for long, when he already took part in his landlords business. But daily, at the hour appointed by her, he visited beautiful Kamala, wearing pretty clothes, fine shoes, and soon he brought her gifts as well. Much he learned from her red, smart mouth. Much he learned from her tender, supple hand. Him, who was, regarding love, still a boy and had a tendency to plunge blindly and insatiably into lust like into a bottomless pit, him she taught, thoroughly starting with the basics, about that school of thought which teaches that pleasure cannot be be taken without giving pleasure, and that every gesture, every caress, every touch, every look, every spot of the body, however small it was, had its secret, which would bring happiness to those who know about it and unleash it. She taught him, that lovers must not part from one another after celebrating love, without one admiring the other, without being just as defeated as they have been victorious, so that with none of them should start feeling fed up or bored and get that evil feeling of having abused or having been abused. Wonderful hours he spent with the beautiful and smart artist, became her student, her lover, her friend. Here with Kamala was the worth and purpose of his present life, nit with the business of Kamaswami.

The merchant passed to duties of writing important letters and contracts on to him and got into the habit of discussing all important affairs with him. He soon saw that Siddhartha knew little about rice and wool, shipping and trade, but that he acted in a fortunate manner, and that Siddhartha surpassed him, the merchant, in calmness and equanimity, and in the art of listening and deeply understanding previously unknown people. "This Brahman," he said to a friend, "is no proper merchant and will never be one, there is never any passion in his soul when he conducts our business. But he has that mysterious quality of those people to whom success comes all by itself, whether this may be a good star of his birth, magic, or something he has learned among Samanas. He always seems to be merely playing with out business-affairs, they never fully become a part of him, they never rule over him, he is never afraid of failure, he is never upset by a loss."

The friend advised the merchant: "Give him from the business he conducts for you a third of the profits, but let him also be liable for the same amount of the losses, when there is a loss. Then, he'll become more zealous."

Kamaswami followed the advice. But Siddhartha cared little about this. When he made a profit, he accepted it with equanimity; when he made losses, he laughed and said: "Well, look at this, so this one turned out badly!"

It seemed indeed, as if he did not care about the business. At one time, he travelled to a village to buy a large harvest of rice there. But when he got there, the rice had already been sold to another merchant. Nevertheless, Siddhartha stayed for several days in that village, treated the farmers for a drink, gave copper-coins to their children, joined in the celebration of a wedding, and returned extremely satisfied from his trip. Kamaswami held against him that he had not turned back right away, that he had wasted time and money. Siddhartha answered: "Stop scolding, dear friend! Nothing was ever achieved by scolding. If a loss has occurred, let me bear that loss. I am very satisfied with this trip. I have gotten to know many kinds of people, a Brahman has become my friend, children have sat on my knees, farmers have shown me their fields, nobody knew that I was a merchant."

"That's all very nice," exclaimed Kamaswami indignantly, "but in fact, you are a merchant after all, one ought to think! Or might you have only travelled for your amusement?"

"Surely," Siddhartha laughed, "surely I have travelled for my amusement. For what else? I have gotten to know people and places, I have received kindness and trust, I have found friendship. Look, my dear, if I had been Kamaswami, I would have travelled back, being annoyed and in a hurry, as soon as I had seen that my purchase had been rendered impossible, and time and money would indeed have been lost. But like this, I've had a few good days, I've learned, had joy, I've neither harmed myself nor others by annoyance and hastiness. And if I'll ever return there again, perhaps to buy an upcoming harvest, or for whatever purpose it might be, friendly people will receive me in a friendly and happy manner, and I will praise myself for not showing any hurry and displeasure at that time. So, leave it as it is, my friend, and don't harm yourself by scolding! If the day will come, when you will see: this Siddhartha is harming me, then speak a word and Siddhartha will go on his own path. But until then, let's be satisfied with one another."

Futile were also the merchant's attempts, to convince Siddhartha that he should eat his bread. Siddhartha ate his own bread, or rather they both ate other people's bread, all people's bread. Siddhartha never listened to Kamaswami's worries and Kamaswami had many worries. Whether there was a business-deal going on which was in danger of failing, or whether a shipment of merchandise seemed to have been lost, or a debtor seemed to be unable to pay, Kamaswami could never convince his partner that it would be useful to utter a few words of worry or anger, to have wrinkles on the forehead, to sleep badly. When, one day, Kamaswami held against him that he had learned everything he knew from him, he replied: "Would you please not kid me with such jokes! What I've learned from you is how much a basket of fish costs and how much interests may be charged on loaned money. These are your areas of expertise. I haven't learned to think from you, my dear Kamaswami, you ought to be the one seeking to learn from me."

Indeed his soul was not with the trade. The business was good enough to provide him with the money for Kamala, and it earned him much more than he needed. Besides from this, Siddhartha's interest and curiosity was only concerned with the people, whose businesses, crafts, worries, pleasures, and acts of foolishness used to be as alien and distant to him as the moon. However easily he succeeded in talking to all of them, in living with all of them, in learning from all of them, he was still aware that there was something which separated him from them and this separating factor was him being a Samana. He saw mankind going trough life in a childlike or animallike manner, which he loved and also despised at the same time. He saw them toiling, saw them suffering, and becoming gray for the sake of things which seemed to him to entirely unworthy of this price, for money, for little pleasures, for being slightly honoured, he saw them scolding and insulting each other, he saw them complaining about pain at which a Samana would only smile, and suffering because of deprivations which a Samana would not feel.

He was open to everything, these people brought his way. Welcome was the merchant who offered him linen for sale, welcome was the debtor who sought another loan, welcome was the beggar who told him for one hour the story of his poverty and who was not half as poor as any given Samana. He did not treat the rich foreign merchant any different than the servant who shaved him and the street-vendor whom he let cheat him out of some small change when buying bananas. When Kamaswami came to him, to complain about his worries or to reproach him concerning his business, he listened curiously and happily, was puzzled by him, tried to understand him, consented that he was a little bit right, only as much as he considered indispensable, and turned away from him, towards the next person who would ask for him. And there were many who came to him, many to do business with him, many to cheat him, many to draw some secret out of him, many to appeal to his sympathy, many to get his advice. He gave advice, he pitied, he made gifts, he let them cheat him a bit, and this entire game and the passion with which all people played this game occupied his thoughts just as much as the gods and Brahmans used to occupy them.

At times he felt, deep in his chest, a dying, quiet voice, which admonished him quietly, lamented quietly; he hardly perceived it. And then, for an hour, he became aware of the strange life he was leading, of him doing lots of things which were only a game, of, though being happy and feeling joy at times, real life still passing him by and not touching him. As a ball-player plays with his balls, he played with his business-deals, with the people around him, watched them, found amusement in them; with his heart, with the source of his being, he was not with them. The source ran somewhere, far away from him, ran and ran invisibly, had nothing to do with his life any more. And at several times he suddenly became scared on account of such thoughts and wished that he would also be gifted with the ability to participate in all of this childlike-naive occupations of the daytime with passion and with his heart, really to live, really to act, really to enjoy and to live instead of just standing by as a spectator. But again and again, he came back to beautiful Kamala, learned the art of love, practised the cult of lust, in which more than in anything else giving and taking becomes one, chatted with her, learned from her, gave her advice, received advice. She understood him better than Govinda used to understand him, she was more similar to him.

Once, he said to her: "You are like me, you are different from most people. You are Kamala, nothing else, and inside of you, there is a peace and refuge, to which you can go at every hour of the day and be at home at yourself, as I can also do. Few people have this, and yet all could have it."

"Not all people are smart," said Kamala.

"No," said Siddhartha, "that's not the reason why. Kamaswami is just as smart as I, and still has no refuge in himself. Others have it, who are small children with respect to their mind. Most people, Kamala, are like a falling leaf, which is blown and is turning around through the air, and wavers, and tumbles to the ground. But others, a few, are like stars, they go on a fixed course, no wind reaches them, in themselves they have their law and their course. Among all the learned men and Samanas, of which I knew many, there was one of this kind, a perfected one, I'll never be able to forget him. It is that Gotama, the exalted one, who is spreading that teachings. Thousands of followers are listening to his teachings every day, follow his instructions every hour, but they are all falling leaves, not in themselves they have teachings and a law."

Kamala looked at him with a smile. "Again, you're talking about him," she said, "again, you're having a Samana's thoughts."

Siddhartha said nothing, and they played the game of love, one of the thirty or forty different games Kamala knew. Her body was flexible like that of a jaguar and like the bow of a hunter; he who had learned from her how to make love, was knowledgeable of many forms of lust, many secrets. For a long time, she played with Siddhartha, enticed him, rejected him, forced him, embraced him: enjoyed his masterful skills, until he was defeated and rested exhausted by her side.

The courtesan bent over him, took a long look at his face, at his eyes, which had grown tired.

"You are the best lover," she said thoughtfully, "I ever saw. You're stronger than others, more supple, more willing. You've learned my art well, Siddhartha. At some time, when I'll be older, I'd want to bear your child. And yet, my dear, you've remained a Samana, and yet you do not love me, you love nobody. Isn't it so?"

"It might very well be so," Siddhartha said tiredly. "I am like you. You also do not love—how else could you practise love as a craft? Perhaps, people of our kind can't love. The childlike people can; that's their secret."

## SANSARA

For a long time, Siddhartha had lived the life of the world and of lust, though without being a part of it. His senses, which he had killed off in hot years as a Samana, had awoken again, he had tasted riches, had tasted lust, had tasted power; nevertheless he had still remained in his heart for a long time a Samana; Kamala, being smart, had realized this quite right. It was still the art of thinking, of waiting, of fasting, which guided his life; still the people of the world, the childlike people, had remained alien to him as he was alien to them.

Years passed by; surrounded by the good life, Siddhartha hardly felt them fading away. He had become rich, for quite a while he possessed a house of his own and his own servants, and a garden before the city by the river. The people liked him, they came to him, whenever they needed money or advice, but there was nobody close to him, except Kamala.

That high, bright state of being awake, which he had experienced that one time at the height of his youth, in those days after Gotama's sermon, after the separation from Govinda, that tense expectation, that proud state of standing alone without teachings and without teachers, that supple willingness to listen to the divine voice in his own heart, had slowly become a memory, had been fleeting; distant and quiet, the holy source murmured, which used to be near, which used to murmur within himself. Nevertheless, many things he had learned from the Samanas, he had learned from Gotama, he had learned from his father the Brahman, had remained within him for a long time afterwards: moderate living, joy of thinking, hours of meditation, secret knowledge of the self, of his eternal entity, which is neither body nor consciousness. Many a part of this he still had, but one part after another had been submerged and had gathered dust. Just as a potter's wheel, once it has been set in motion, will keep on turning for a long time and only slowly lose its vigour and come to a stop, thus Siddhartha's soul had kept on turning the wheel of asceticism, the wheel of thinking, the wheel of differentiation for a long time, still turning, but it turned slowly and hesitantly and was close to coming to a standstill. Slowly, like humidity entering the dying stem of a tree, filling it slowly and making it rot, the world and sloth had entered Siddhartha's soul, slowly it filled his soul, made it heavy, made it tired, put it to sleep. On the other hand, his senses had become alive, there was much they had learned, much they had experienced.

Siddhartha had learned to trade, to use his power over people, to enjoy himself with a woman, he had learned to wear beautiful clothes, to give orders to servants, to bathe in perfumed waters. He had learned to eat tenderly and carefully prepared food, even fish, even meat and poultry, spices and sweets, and to drink wine, which causes sloth and forgetfulness. He had learned to play with dice and on a chess-board, to watch dancing girls, to have himself carried about in a sedan-chair, to sleep on a soft bed. But still he had felt different from and superior to the others; always he had watched them with some mockery, some mocking disdain, with the same disdain which a Samana constantly feels for the people of the world. When Kamaswami was ailing, when he was annoyed, when he felt insulted, when he was vexed by his worries as a merchant, Siddhartha had always watched it with mockery. Just slowly and imperceptibly, as the harvest seasons and rainy seasons passed by, his mockery had become more tired, his superiority had become more quiet. Just slowly, among his growing riches, Siddhartha had assumed something of the childlike people's ways for himself, something of their childlikeness and of their fearfulness. And yet, he envied them, envied them just the more, the more similar he became to them. He envied them for the one thing that was missing from him and that they had, the importance they were able to attach to their lives, the amount of passion in their joys and fears, the fearful but sweet happiness of being constantly in love. These people were all of the time in love with themselves, with women, with their children, with honours or money, with plans or hopes. But he did not learn this from them, this out of all things, this joy of a child and this foolishness of a child; he learned from them out of all things the unpleasant ones, which he himself despised. It happened more and more often that, in the morning after having had company the night before, he stayed in bed for a long time, felt unable to think and tired. It happened that he became angry and impatient, when Kamaswami bored him with his worries. It happened that he laughed just too loud, when he lost a game of dice. His face was still smarter and more spiritual than others, but it rarely laughed, and assumed, one after another, those features which are so often found in the faces of rich people, those features of discontent, of sickliness, of ill-humour, of sloth, of a lack of love. Slowly the disease of the soul, which rich people have, grabbed hold of him.

Like a veil, like a thin mist, tiredness came over Siddhartha, slowly, getting a bit denser every day, a bit murkier every month, a bit heavier every year. As a new dress becomes old in time, loses its beautiful colour in time, gets stains, gets wrinkles, gets worn off at the seams, and starts to show threadbare spots here and there, thus Siddhartha's new life, which he had started after his separation from Govinda, had grown old, lost colour and splendour as the years passed by, was gathering wrinkles and stains, and hidden at bottom, already showing its ugliness here and there, disappointment and disgust were waiting. Siddhartha did not notice it. He only noticed that this bright and reliable voice inside of him, which had awoken in him at that time and had ever guided him in his best times, had become silent.

He had been captured by the world, by lust, covetousness, sloth, and finally also by that vice which he had used to despise and mock the most as the most foolish one of all vices: greed. Property, possessions, and riches also had finally captured him; they were no longer a game and trifles to him, had become a shackle and a burden. On a strange and devious way, Siddhartha had gotten into this final and most base of all dependencies, by means of the game of dice. It was since that time, when he had stopped being a Samana in his heart, that Siddhartha began to play the game for money and precious things, which he at other times only joined with a smile and casually as a custom of the childlike people, with an increasing rage and passion. He was a feared gambler, few dared to take him on, so high and audacious were his stakes. He played the game due to a pain of his heart, losing and wasting his wretched money in the game brought him an angry joy, in no other way he could demonstrate his disdain for wealth, the merchants' false god, more clearly and more mockingly. Thus he gambled with high stakes and mercilessly, hating himself, mocking himself, won thousands, threw away thousands, lost money, lost jewelry, lost a house in the country, won again, lost again. That fear, that terrible and petrifying fear, which he felt while he was rolling the dice, while he was worried about losing high stakes, that fear he loved and sought to always renew it, always increase it, always get it to a slightly higher level, for in this feeling alone he still felt something like happiness, something like an intoxication, something like an elevated form of life in the midst of his saturated, lukewarm, dull life.

And after each big loss, his mind was set on new riches, pursued the trade more zealously, forced his debtors more strictly to pay, because he wanted to continue gambling, he wanted to continue squandering, continue demonstrating his disdain of wealth. Siddhartha lost his calmness when losses occurred, lost his patience when he was not payed on time, lost his kindness towards beggars, lost his disposition for giving away and loaning money to those who petitioned him. He, who gambled away tens of thousands at one roll of the dice and laughed at it, became more strict and more petty in his business, occasionally dreaming at night about money! And whenever he woke up from this ugly spell, whenever he found his face in the mirror at the bedroom's wall to have aged and become more ugly, whenever embarrassment and disgust came over him, he continued fleeing, fleeing into a new game, fleeing into a numbing of his mind brought on by sex, by wine, and from there he fled back into the urge to pile up and obtain possessions. In this pointless cycle he ran, growing tired, growing old, growing ill.

Then the time came when a dream warned him. He had spend the hours of the evening with Kamala, in her beautiful pleasure-garden. They had been sitting under the trees, talking, and Kamala had said thoughtful words, words behind which a sadness and tiredness lay hidden. She had asked him to tell her about Gotama, and could not hear enough of him, how clear his eyes, how still and beautiful his mouth, how kind his smile, how peaceful his walk had been. For a long time, he had to tell her about the exalted Buddha, and Kamala had sighed and had said: "One day, perhaps soon, I'll also follow that Buddha. I'll give him my pleasure-garden for a gift and take my refuge in his teachings." But after this, she had aroused him, and had tied him to her in the act of making love with painful fervour, biting and in tears, as if, once more, she wanted to squeeze the last sweet drop out of this vain, fleeting pleasure. Never before, it had become so strangely clear to Siddhartha, how closely lust was akin to death. Then he had lain by her side, and Kamala's face had been close to him, and under her eyes and next to the corners of her mouth he had, as clearly as never before, read a fearful inscription, an inscription of small lines, of slight grooves, an inscription reminiscent of autumn and old age, just as Siddhartha himself, who was only in his forties, had already noticed, here and there, gray hairs among his black ones. Tiredness was written on Kamala's beautiful face, tiredness from walking a long path, which has no happy destination, tiredness and the beginning of withering, and concealed, still unsaid, perhaps not even conscious anxiety: fear of old age, fear of the autumn, fear of having to die. With a sigh, he had bid his farewell to her, the soul full of reluctance, and full of concealed anxiety.

Then, Siddhartha had spent the night in his house with dancing girls and wine, had acted as if he was superior to them towards the fellow-members of his caste, though this was no longer true, had drunk much wine and gone to bed a long time after midnight, being tired and yet excited, close to weeping and despair, and had for a long time sought to sleep in vain, his heart full of misery which he thought he could not bear any longer, full of a disgust which he felt penetrating his entire body like the lukewarm, repulsive taste of the wine, the just too sweet, dull music, the just too soft smile of the dancing girls, the just too sweet scent of their hair and breasts. But more than by anything else, he was disgusted by himself, by his perfumed hair, by the smell of wine from his mouth, by the flabby tiredness and listlessness of his skin. Like when someone, who has eaten and drunk far too much, vomits it back up again with agonising pain and is nevertheless glad about the relief, thus this sleepless man wished to free himself of these pleasures, these habits and all of this pointless life and himself, in an immense burst of disgust. Not until the light of the morning and the beginning of the first activities in the street before his city-house, he had slightly fallen asleep, had found for a few moments a half unconsciousness, a hint of sleep. In those moments, he had a dream:

Kamala owned a small, rare singing bird in a golden cage. Of this bird, he dreamt. He dreamt: this bird had become mute, who at other times always used to sing in the morning, and since this arose his attention, he stepped in front of the cage and looked inside; there the small bird was dead and lay stiff on the ground. He took it out, weighed it for a moment in his hand, and then threw it away, out in the street, and in the same moment, he felt terribly shocked, and his heart hurt, as if he had thrown away from himself all value and everything good by throwing out this dead bird.

Starting up from this dream, he felt encompassed by a deep sadness. Worthless, so it seemed to him, worthless and pointless was the way he had been going through life; nothing which was alive, nothing which was in some way delicious or worth keeping he had left in his hands. Alone he stood there and empty like a castaway on the shore.

With a gloomy mind, Siddhartha went to the pleasure-garden he owned, locked the gate, sat down under a mango-tree, felt death in his heart and horror in his chest, sat and sensed how everything died in him, withered in him, came to an end in him. By and by, he gathered his thoughts, and in his mind, he once again went the entire path of his life, starting with the first days he could remember. When was there ever a time when he had experienced happiness, felt a true bliss? Oh yes, several times he had experienced such a thing. In his years as a boy, he has had a taste of it, when he had obtained praise from the Brahmans, he had felt it in his heart: "There is a path in front of the one who has distinguished himself in the recitation of the holy verses, in the dispute with the learned ones, as an assistant in the offerings." Then, he had felt it in his heart: "There is a path in front of you, you are destined for, the gods are awaiting you." And again, as a young man, when the ever rising, upward fleeing, goal of all thinking had ripped him out of and up from the multitude of those seeking the same goal, when he wrestled in pain for the purpose of Brahman, when every obtained knowledge only kindled new thirst in him, then again he had, in the midst of the thirst, in the midst of the pain felt this very same thing: "Go on! Go on! You are called upon!" He had heard this voice when he had left his home and had chosen the life of a Samana, and again when he had gone away from the Samanas to that perfected one, and also when he had gone away from him to the uncertain. For how long had he not heard this voice any more, for how long had he reached no height any more, how even and dull was the manner in which his path had passed through life, for many long years, without a high goal, without thirst, without elevation, content with small lustful pleasures and yet never satisfied! For all of these many years, without knowing it himself, he had tried hard and longed to become a man like those many, like those children, and in all this, his life had been much more miserable and poorer than theirs, and their goals were not his, nor their worries; after all, that entire world of the Kamaswami-people had only been a game to him, a dance he would watch, a comedy. Only Kamala had been dear, had been valuable to him—but was she still thus? Did he still need her, or she him? Did they not play a game without an ending? Was it necessary to live for this? No, it was not necessary! The name of this game was Sansara, a game for children, a game which was perhaps enjoyable to play once, twice, ten times—but for ever and ever over again?

Then, Siddhartha knew that the game was over, that he could not play it any more. Shivers ran over his body, inside of him, so he felt, something had died.

That entire day, he sat under the mango-tree, thinking of his father, thinking of Govinda, thinking of Gotama. Did he have to leave them to become a Kamaswami? He still sat there, when the night had fallen. When, looking up, he caught sight of the stars, he thought: "Here I'm sitting under my mango-tree, in my pleasure-garden." He smiled a little —was it really necessary, was it right, was it not as foolish game, that he owned a mango-tree, that he owned a garden?

He also put an end to this, this also died in him. He rose, bid his farewell to the mango-tree, his farewell to the pleasure-garden. Since he had been without food this day, he felt strong hunger, and thought of his house in the city, of his chamber and bed, of the table with the meals on it. He smiled tiredly, shook himself, and bid his farewell to these things.

In the same hour of the night, Siddhartha left his garden, left the city, and never came back. For a long time, Kamaswami had people look for him, thinking that he had fallen into the hands of robbers. Kamala had no one look for him. When she was told that Siddhartha had disappeared, she was not astonished. Did she not always expect it? Was he not a Samana, a man who was at home nowhere, a pilgrim? And most of all, she had felt this the last time they had been together, and she was happy, in spite of all the pain of the loss, that she had pulled him so affectionately to her heart for this last time, that she had felt one more time to be so completely possessed and penetrated by him.

When she received the first news of Siddhartha's disappearance, she went to the window, where she held a rare singing bird captive in a golden cage. She opened the door of the cage, took the bird out and let it fly. For a long time, she gazed after it, the flying bird. From this day on, she received no more visitors and kept her house locked. But after some time, she became aware that she was pregnant from the last time she was together with Siddhartha.

## BY THE RIVER

Siddhartha walked through the forest, was already far from the city, and knew nothing but that one thing, that there was no going back for him, that this life, as he had lived it for many years until now, was over and done away with, and that he had tasted all of it, sucked everything out of it until he was disgusted with it. Dead was the singing bird, he had dreamt of. Dead was the bird in his heart. Deeply, he had been entangled in Sansara, he had sucked up disgust and death from all sides into his body, like a sponge sucks up water until it is full. And full he was, full of the feeling of been sick of it, full of misery, full of death, there was nothing left in this world which could have attracted him, given him joy, given him comfort.

Passionately he wished to know nothing about himself anymore, to have rest, to be dead. If there only was a lightning-bolt to strike him dead! If there only was a tiger a devour him! If there only was a wine, a poison which would numb his senses, bring him forgetfulness and sleep, and no awakening from that! Was there still any kind of filth, he had not soiled himself with, a sin or foolish act he had not committed, a dreariness of the soul he had not brought upon himself? Was it still at all possible to be alive? Was it possible, to breathe in again and again, to breathe out, to feel hunger, to eat again, to sleep again, to sleep with a woman again? Was this cycle not exhausted and brought to a conclusion for him?

Siddhartha reached the large river in the forest, the same river over which a long time ago, when he had still been a young man and came from the town of Gotama, a ferryman had conducted him. By this river he stopped, hesitantly he stood at the bank. Tiredness and hunger had weakened him, and whatever for should he walk on, wherever to, to which goal? No, there were no more goals, there was nothing left but the deep, painful yearning to shake off this whole desolate dream, to spit out this stale wine, to put an end to this miserable and shameful life.

A hang bent over the bank of the river, a coconut-tree; Siddhartha leaned against its trunk with his shoulder, embraced the trunk with one arm, and looked down into the green water, which ran and ran under him, looked down and found himself to be entirely filled with the wish to let go and to drown in these waters. A frightening emptiness was reflected back at him by the water, answering to the terrible emptiness in his soul. Yes, he had reached the end. There was nothing left for him, except to annihilate himself, except to smash the failure into which he had shaped his life, to throw it away, before the feet of mockingly laughing gods. This was the great vomiting he had longed for: death, the smashing to bits of the form he hated! Let him be food for fishes, this dog Siddhartha, this lunatic, this depraved and rotten body, this weakened and abused soul! Let him be food for fishes and crocodiles, let him be chopped to bits by the daemons!

With a distorted face, he stared into the water, saw the reflection of his face and spit at it. In deep tiredness, he took his arm away from the trunk of the tree and turned a bit, in order to let himself fall straight down, in order to finally drown. With his eyes closed, he slipped towards death.

Then, out of remote areas of his soul, out of past times of his now weary life, a sound stirred up. It was a word, a syllable, which he, without thinking, with a slurred voice, spoke to himself, the old word which is the beginning and the end of all prayers of the Brahmans, the holy "Om", which roughly means "that what is perfect" or "the completion". And in the moment when the sound of "Om" touched Siddhartha's ear, his dormant spirit suddenly woke up and realized the foolishness of his actions.

Siddhartha was deeply shocked. So this was how things were with him, so doomed was he, so much he had lost his way and was forsaken by all knowledge, that he had been able to seek death, that this wish, this wish of a child, had been able to grow in him: to find rest by annihilating his body! What all agony of these recent times, all sobering realizations, all desperation had not brought about, this was brought on by this moment, when the Om entered his consciousness: he became aware of himself in his misery and in his error.

Om! he spoke to himself: Om! and again he knew about Brahman, knew about the indestructibility of life, knew about all that is divine, which he had forgotten.

But this was only a moment, flash. By the foot of the coconut-tree, Siddhartha collapsed, struck down by tiredness, mumbling Om, placed his head on the root of the tree and fell into a deep sleep.

Deep was his sleep and without dreams, for a long time he had not known such a sleep any more. When he woke up after many hours, he felt as if ten years had passed, he heard the water quietly flowing, did not know where he was and who had brought him here, opened his eyes, saw with astonishment that there were trees and the sky above him, and he remembered where he was and how he got here. But it took him a long while for this, and the past seemed to him as if it had been covered by a veil, infinitely distant, infinitely far away, infinitely meaningless. He only knew that his previous life (in the first moment when he thought about it, this past life seemed to him like a very old, previous incarnation, like an early pre-birth of his present self)—that his previous life had been abandoned by him, that, full of disgust and wretchedness, he had even intended to throw his life away, but that by a river, under a coconut-tree, he has come to his senses, the holy word Om on his lips, that then he had fallen asleep and had now woken up and was looking at the world as a new man. Quietly, he spoke the word Om to himself, speaking which he had fallen asleep, and it seemed to him as if his entire long sleep had been nothing but a long meditative recitation of Om, a thinking of Om, a submergence and complete entering into Om, into the nameless, the perfected.

What a wonderful sleep had this been! Never before by sleep, he had been thus refreshed, thus renewed, thus rejuvenated! Perhaps, he had really died, had drowned and was reborn in a new body? But no, he knew himself, he knew his hand and his feet, knew the place where he lay, knew this self in his chest, this Siddhartha, the eccentric, the weird one, but this Siddhartha was nevertheless transformed, was renewed, was strangely well rested, strangely awake, joyful and curious.

Siddhartha straightened up, then he saw a person sitting opposite to him, an unknown man, a monk in a yellow robe with a shaven head, sitting in the position of pondering. He observed the man, who had neither hair on his head nor a beard, and he had not observed him for long when he recognised this monk as Govinda, the friend of his youth, Govinda who had taken his refuge with the exalted Buddha. Govinda had aged, he too, but still his face bore the same features, expressed zeal, faithfulness, searching, timidness. But when Govinda now, sensing his gaze, opened his eyes and looked at him, Siddhartha saw that Govinda did not recognise him. Govinda was happy to find him awake; apparently, he had been sitting here for a long time and been waiting for him to wake up, though he did not know him.

"I have been sleeping," said Siddhartha. "However did you get here?"

"You have been sleeping," answered Govinda. "It is not good to be sleeping in such places, where snakes often are and the animals of the forest have their paths. I, oh sir, am a follower of the exalted Gotama, the Buddha, the Sakyamuni, and have been on a pilgrimage together with several of us on this path, when I saw you lying and sleeping in a place where it is dangerous to sleep. Therefore, I sought to wake you up, oh sir, and since I saw that your sleep was very deep, I stayed behind from my group and sat with you. And then, so it seems, I have fallen asleep myself, I who wanted to guard your sleep. Badly, I have served you, tiredness has overwhelmed me. But now that you're awake, let me go to catch up with my brothers."

"I thank you, Samana, for watching out over my sleep," spoke Siddhartha. "You're friendly, you followers of the exalted one. Now you may go then."

"I'm going, sir. May you, sir, always be in good health."

"I thank you, Samana."

Govinda made the gesture of a salutation and said: "Farewell."

"Farewell, Govinda," said Siddhartha.

The monk stopped.

"Permit me to ask, sir, from where do you know my name?"

Now, Siddhartha smiled.

"I know you, oh Govinda, from your father's hut, and from the school of the Brahmans, and from the offerings, and from our walk to the Samanas, and from that hour when you took your refuge with the exalted one in the grove Jetavana."

"You're Siddhartha," Govinda exclaimed loudly. "Now, I'm recognising you, and don't comprehend any more how I couldn't recognise you right away. Be welcome, Siddhartha, my joy is great, to see you again."

"It also gives me joy, to see you again. You've been the guard of my sleep, again I thank you for this, though I wouldn't have required any guard. Where are you going to, oh friend?"

"I'm going nowhere. We monks are always travelling, whenever it is not the rainy season, we always move from one place to another, live according to the rules if the teachings passed on to us, accept alms, move on. It is always like this. But you,

Siddhartha, where are you going to?"

Quoth Siddhartha: "With me too, friend, it is as it is with you. I'm going nowhere. I'm just travelling. I'm on a pilgrimage."

Govinda spoke: "You're saying: you're on a pilgrimage, and I believe in you. But, forgive me, oh Siddhartha, you do not look like a pilgrim. You're wearing a rich man's garments, you're wearing the shoes of a distinguished gentleman, and your hair, with the fragrance of perfume, is not a pilgrim's hair, not the hair of a Samana."

"Right so, my dear, you have observed well, your keen eyes see everything. But I haven't said to you that I was a Samana. I said: I'm on a pilgrimage. And so it is: I'm on a pilgrimage."

"You're on a pilgrimage," said Govinda. "But few would go on a pilgrimage in such clothes, few in such shoes, few with such hair. Never I have met such a pilgrim, being a pilgrim myself for many years."

"I believe you, my dear Govinda. But now, today, you've met a pilgrim just like this, wearing such shoes, such a garment. Remember, my dear: Not eternal is the world of appearances, not eternal, anything but eternal are our garments and the style of our hair, and our hair and bodies themselves. I'm wearing a rich man's clothes, you've seen this quite right. I'm wearing them, because I have been a rich man, and I'm wearing my hair like the worldly and lustful people, for I have been one of them."

"And now, Siddhartha, what are you now?"

"I don't know it, I don't know it just like you. I'm travelling. I was a rich man and am no rich man any more, and what I'll be tomorrow, I don't know."

"You've lost your riches?"

"I've lost them or they me. They somehow happened to slip away from me. The wheel of physical manifestations is turning quickly, Govinda. Where is Siddhartha the Brahman? Where is Siddhartha the Samana? Where is Siddhartha the rich man? Non-eternal things change quickly, Govinda, you know it."

Govinda looked at the friend of his youth for a long time, with doubt in his eyes. After that, he gave him the salutation which one would use on a gentleman and went on his way.

With a smiling face, Siddhartha watched him leave, he loved him still, this faithful man, this fearful man. And how could he not have loved everybody and everything in this moment, in the glorious hour after his wonderful sleep, filled with Om! The enchantment, which had happened inside of him in his sleep and by means of the Om, was this very thing that he loved everything, that he was full of joyful love for everything he saw. And it was this very thing, so it seemed to him now, which had been his sickness before, that he was not able to love anybody or anything.

With a smiling face, Siddhartha watched the leaving monk. The sleep had strengthened him much, but hunger gave him much pain, for by now he had not eaten for two days, and the times were long past when he had been tough against hunger. With sadness, and yet also with a smile, he thought of that time. In those days, so he remembered, he had boasted of three three things to Kamala, had been able to do three noble and undefeatable feats: fasting—waiting—thinking. These had been his possession, his power and strength, his solid staff; in the busy, laborious years of his youth, he had learned these three feats, nothing else. And now, they had abandoned him, none of them was his any more, neither fasting, nor waiting, nor thinking. For the most wretched things, he had given them up, for what fades most quickly, for sensual lust, for the good life, for riches! His life had indeed been strange. And now, so it seemed, now he had really become a childlike person.

Siddhartha thought about his situation. Thinking was hard on him, he did not really feel like it, but he forced himself.

Now, he thought, since all these most easily perishing things have slipped from me again, now I'm standing here under the sun again just as I have been standing here a little child, nothing is mine, I have no abilities, there is nothing I could bring about, I have learned nothing. How wondrous is this! Now, that I'm no longer young, that my hair is already half gray, that my strength is fading, now I'm starting again at the beginning and as a child! Again, he had to smile. Yes, his fate had been strange! Things were going downhill with him, and now he was again facing the world void and naked and stupid. But he could not feed sad about this, no, he even felt a great urge to laugh, to laugh about himself, to laugh about this strange, foolish world.

"Things are going downhill with you!" he said to himself, and laughed about it, and as he was saying it, he happened to glance at the river, and he also saw the river going downhill, always moving on downhill, and singing and being happy through it all. He liked this well, kindly he smiled at the river. Was this not the river in which he had intended to drown himself, in past times, a hundred years ago, or had he dreamed this?

Wondrous indeed was my life, so he thought, wondrous detours it has taken. As I boy, I had only to do with gods and offerings. As a youth, I had only to do with asceticism, with thinking and meditation, was searching for Brahman, worshipped the eternal in the Atman. But as a young man, I followed the penitents, lived in the forest, suffered of heat and frost, learned to hunger, taught my body to become dead. Wonderfully, soon afterwards, insight came towards me in the form of the great Buddha's teachings, I felt the knowledge of the oneness of the world circling in me like my own blood. But I also had to leave Buddha and the great knowledge. I went and learned the art of love with Kamala, learned trading with Kamaswami, piled up money, wasted money, learned to love my stomach, learned to please my senses. I had to spend many years losing my spirit, to unlearn thinking again, to forget the oneness. Isn't it just as if I had turned slowly and on a long detour from a man into a child, from a thinker into a childlike person? And yet, this path has been very good; and yet, the bird in my chest has not died. But what a path has this been! I had to pass through so much stupidity, through so much vices, through so many errors, through so much disgust and disappointments and woe, just to become a child again and to be able to start over. But it was right so, my heart says "Yes" to it, my eyes smile to it. I've had to experience despair, I've had to sink down to the most foolish one of all thoughts, to the thought of suicide, in order to be able to experience divine grace, to hear Om again, to be able to sleep properly and awake properly again. I had to become a fool, to find Atman in me again. I had to sin, to be able to live again. Where else might my path lead me to? It is foolish, this path, it moves in loops, perhaps it is going around in a circle. Let it go as it likes, I want to to take it.

Wonderfully, he felt joy rolling like waves in his chest.

Wherever from, he asked his heart, where from did you get this happiness? Might it come from that long, good sleep, which has done me so good? Or from the word Om, which I said? Or from the fact that I have escaped, that I have completely fled, that I am finally free again and am standing like a child under the sky? Oh how good is it to have fled, to have become free! How clean and beautiful is the air here, how good to breathe! There, where I ran away from, there everything smelled of ointments, of spices, of wine, of excess, of sloth. How did I hate this world of the rich, of those who revel in fine food, of the gamblers! How did I hate myself for staying in this terrible world for so long! How did I hate myself, have deprive, poisoned, tortured myself, have made myself old and evil! No, never again I will, as I used to like doing so much, delude myself into thinking that Siddhartha was wise! But this one thing I have done well, this I like, this I must praise, that there is now an end to that hatred against myself, to that foolish and dreary life! I praise you, Siddhartha, after so many years of foolishness, you have once again had an idea, have done something, have heard the bird in your chest singing and have followed it!

Thus he praised himself, found joy in himself, listened curiously to his stomach, which was rumbling with hunger. He had now, so he felt, in these recent times and days, completely tasted and spit out, devoured up to the point of desperation and death, a piece of suffering, a piece of misery. Like this, it was good. For much longer, he could have stayed with Kamaswami, made money, wasted money, filled his stomach, and let his soul die of thirst; for much longer he could have lived in this soft, well upholstered hell, if this had not happened: the moment of complete hopelessness and despair, that most extreme moment, when he hang over the rushing waters and was ready to destroy himself. That he had felt this despair, this deep disgust, and that he had not succumbed to it, that the bird, the joyful source and voice in him was still alive after all, this was why he felt joy, this was why he laughed, this was why his face was smiling brightly under his hair which had turned gray.

"It is good," he thought, "to get a taste of everything for oneself, which one needs to know. That lust for the world and riches do not belong to the good things, I have already learned as a child. I have known it for a long time, but I have experienced only now. And now I know it, don't just know it in my memory, but in my eyes, in my heart, in my stomach. Good for me, to know this!"

For a long time, he pondered his transformation, listened to the bird, as it sang for joy. Had not this bird died in him, had he not felt its death? No, something else from within him had died, something which already for a long time had yearned to die. Was it not this what he used to intend to kill in his ardent years as a penitent? Was this not his self, his small, frightened, and proud self, he had wrestled with for so many years, which had defeated him again and again, which was back again after every killing, prohibited joy, felt fear? Was it not this, which today had finally come to its death, here in the forest, by this lovely river? Was it not due to this death, that he was now like a child, so full of trust, so without fear, so full of joy?

Now Siddhartha also got some idea of why he had fought this self in vain as a Brahman, as a penitent. Too much knowledge had held him back, too many holy verses, too many sacrificial rules, to much self-castigation, so much doing and striving for that goal! Full of arrogance, he had been, always the smartest, always working the most, always one step ahead of all others, always the knowing and spiritual one, always the priest or wise one. Into being a priest, into this arrogance, into this spirituality, his self had retreated, there it sat firmly and grew, while he thought he would kill it by fasting and penance. Now he saw it and saw that the secret voice had been right, that no teacher would ever have been able to bring about his salvation. Therefore, he had to go out into the world, lose himself to lust and power, to woman and money, had to become a merchant, a dice-gambler, a drinker, and a greedy person, until the priest and Samana in him was dead. Therefore, he had to continue bearing these ugly years, bearing the disgust, the teachings, the pointlessness of a dreary and wasted life up to the end, up to bitter despair, until Siddhartha the lustful, Siddhartha the greedy could also die. He had died, a new Siddhartha had woken up from the sleep. He would also grow old, he would also eventually have to die, mortal was Siddhartha, mortal was every physical form. But today he was young, was a child, the new Siddhartha, and was full of joy.

He thought these thoughts, listened with a smile to his stomach, listened gratefully to a buzzing bee. Cheerfully, he looked into the rushing river, never before he had like a water so well as this one, never before he had perceived the voice and the parable of the moving water thus strongly and beautifully. It seemed to him, as if the river had something special to tell him, something he did not know yet, which was still awaiting him. In this river, Siddhartha had intended to drown himself, in it the old, tired, desperate Siddhartha had drowned today. But the new Siddhartha felt a deep love for this rushing water, and decided for himself, not to leave it very soon.

# THE FERRYMAN

By this river I want to stay, thought Siddhartha, it is the same which I have crossed a long time ago on my way to the childlike people, a friendly ferryman had guided me then, he is the one I want to go to, starting out from his hut, my path had led me at that time into a new life, which had now grown old and is dead—my present path, my present new life, shall also take its start there!

Tenderly, he looked into the rushing water, into the transparent green, into the crystal lines of its drawing, so rich in secrets. Bright pearls he saw rising from the deep, quiet bubbles of air floating on the reflecting surface, the blue of the sky being depicted in it. With a thousand eyes, the river looked at him, with green ones, with white ones, with crystal ones, with sky-blue ones. How did he love this water, how did it delight him, how grateful was he to it! In his heart he heard the voice talking, which was newly awaking, and it told him: Love this water! Stay near it! Learn from it! Oh yes, he wanted to learn from it, he wanted to listen to it. He who would understand this water and its secrets, so it seemed to him, would also understand many other things, many secrets, all secrets.

But out of all secrets of the river, he today only saw one, this one touched his soul. He saw: this water ran and ran, incessantly it ran, and was nevertheless always there, was always at all times the same and yet new in every moment! Great be he who would grasp this, understand this! He understood and grasped it not, only felt some idea of it stirring, a distant memory, divine voices.

Siddhartha rose, the workings of hunger in his body became unbearable. In a daze he walked on, up the path by the bank, upriver, listened to the current, listened to the rumbling hunger in his body.

When he reached the ferry, the boat was just ready, and the same ferryman who had once transported the young Samana across the river, stood in the boat, Siddhartha recognised him, he had also aged very much.

"Would you like to ferry me over?" he asked.

The ferryman, being astonished to see such an elegant man walking along and on foot, took him into his boat and pushed it off the bank.

"It's a beautiful life you have chosen for yourself," the passenger spoke. "It must be beautiful to live by this water every day and to cruise on it."

With a smile, the man at the oar moved from side to side: "It is beautiful, sir, it is as you say. But isn't every life, isn't every work beautiful?"

"This may be true. But I envy you for yours."

"Ah, you would soon stop enjoying it. This is nothing for people wearing fine clothes."

Siddhartha laughed. "Once before, I have been looked upon today because of my clothes, I have been looked upon with distrust. Wouldn't you, ferryman, like to accept these clothes, which are a nuisance to me, from me? For you must know, I have no money to pay your fare."

"You're joking, sir," the ferryman laughed.

"I'm not joking, friend. Behold, once before you have ferried me across this water in your boat for the immaterial reward of a good deed. Thus, do it today as well, and accept my clothes for it."

"And do you, sir, intent to continue travelling without clothes?"

"Ah, most of all I wouldn't want to continue travelling at all. Most of all I would like you, ferryman, to give me an old loincloth and kept me with you as your assistant, or rather as your trainee, for I'll have to learn first how to handle the boat."

For a long time, the ferryman looked at the stranger, searching.

"Now I recognise you," he finally said. "At one time, you've slept in my hut, this was a long time ago, possibly more than twenty years ago, and you've been ferried across the river by me, and we parted like good friends. Haven't you've been a Samana? I can't think of your name any more."

"My name is Siddhartha, and I was a Samana, when you've last seen me."

"So be welcome, Siddhartha. My name is Vasudeva. You will, so I hope, be my guest today as well and sleep in my hut, and tell me, where you're coming from and why these beautiful clothes are such a nuisance to you."

They had reached the middle of the river, and Vasudeva pushed the oar with more strength, in order to overcome the current. He worked calmly, his eyes fixed in on the front of the boat, with brawny arms. Siddhartha sat and watched him, and remembered, how once before, on that last day of his time as a Samana, love for this man had stirred in his heart. Gratefully, he accepted Vasudeva's invitation. When they had reached the bank, he helped him to tie the boat to the stakes; after this, the ferryman asked him to enter the hut, offered him bread and water, and Siddhartha ate with eager pleasure, and also ate with eager pleasure of the mango fruits, Vasudeva offered him.

Afterwards, it was almost the time of the sunset, they sat on a log by the bank, and Siddhartha told the ferryman about where he originally came from and about his life, as he had seen it before his eyes today, in that hour of despair. Until late at night, lasted his tale.

Vasudeva listened with great attention. Listening carefully, he let everything enter his mind, birthplace and childhood, all that learning, all that searching, all joy, all distress. This was among the ferryman's virtues one of the greatest: like only a few, he knew how to listen. Without him having spoken a word, the speaker sensed how Vasudeva let his words enter his mind, quiet, open, waiting, how he did not lose a single one, awaited not a single one with impatience, did not add his praise or rebuke, was just listening. Siddhartha felt, what a happy fortune it is, to confess to such a listener, to bury in his heart his own life, his own search, his own suffering.

But in the end of Siddhartha's tale, when he spoke of the tree by the river, and of his deep fall, of the holy Om, and how he had felt such a love for the river after his slumber, the ferryman listened with twice the attention, entirely and completely absorbed by it, with his eyes closed.

But when Siddhartha fell silent, and a long silence had occurred, then Vasudeva said: "It is as I thought. The river has spoken to you. It is your friend as well, it speaks to you as well. That is good, that is very good. Stay with me, Siddhartha, my friend. I used to have a wife, her bed was next to mine, but she has died a long time ago, for a long time, I have lived alone. Now, you shall live with me, there is space and food for both."

"I thank you," said Siddhartha, "I thank you and accept. And I also thank you for this, Vasudeva, for listening to me so well! These people are rare who know how to listen. And I did not meet a single one who knew it as well as you did. I will also learn in this respect from you."

"You will learn it," spoke Vasudeva, "but not from me. The river has taught me to listen, from it you will learn it as well. It knows everything, the river, everything can be learned from it. See, you've already learned this from the water too, that it is good to strive downwards, to sink, to seek depth. The rich and elegant Siddhartha is becoming an oarsman's servant, the learned Brahman Siddhartha becomes a ferryman: this has also been told to you by the river. You'll learn that other thing from it as well."

Quoth Siddhartha after a long pause: "What other thing, Vasudeva?"

Vasudeva rose. "It is late," he said, "let's go to sleep. I can't tell you that other thing, oh friend. You'll learn it, or perhaps you know it already. See, I'm no learned man, I have no special skill in speaking, I also have no special skill in thinking. All I'm able to do is to listen and to be godly, I have learned nothing else. If I was able to say and teach it, I might be a wise man, but like this I am only a ferryman, and it is my task to ferry people across the river. I have transported many, thousands; and to all of them, my river has been nothing but an obstacle on their travels. They travelled to seek money and business, and for weddings, and on pilgrimages, and the river was obstructing their path, and the ferryman's job was to get them quickly across that obstacle. But for some among thousands, a few, four or five, the river has stopped being an obstacle, they have heard its voice, they have listened to it, and the river has become sacred to them, as it has become sacred to me. Let's rest now, Siddhartha."

Siddhartha stayed with the ferryman and learned to operate the boat, and when there was nothing to do at the ferry, he worked with Vasudeva in the rice-field, gathered wood, plucked the fruit off the banana-trees. He learned to build an oar, and learned to mend the boat, and to weave baskets, and was joyful because of everything he learned, and the days and months passed quickly. But more than Vasudeva could teach him, he was taught by the river. Incessantly, he learned from it. Most of all, he learned from it to listen, to pay close attention with a quiet heart, with a waiting, opened soul, without passion, without a wish, without judgement, without an opinion.

In a friendly manner, he lived side by side with Vasudeva, and occasionally they exchanged some words, few and at length thought about words. Vasudeva was no friend of words; rarely, Siddhartha succeeded in persuading him to speak.

"Did you," so he asked him at one time, "did you too learn that secret from the river: that there is no time?"

Vasudeva's face was filled with a bright smile.

"Yes, Siddhartha," he spoke. "It is this what you mean, isn't it: that the river is everywhere at once, at the source and at the mouth, at the waterfall, at the ferry, at the rapids, in the sea, in the mountains, everywhere at once, and that there is only the present time for it, not the shadow of the past, not the shadow of the future?"

"This it is," said Siddhartha. "And when I had learned it, I looked at my life, and it was also a river, and the boy Siddhartha was only separated from the man Siddhartha and from the old man Siddhartha by a shadow, not by something real. Also, Siddhartha's previous births were no past, and his death and his return to Brahma was no future. Nothing was, nothing will be; everything is, everything has existence and is present."

Siddhartha spoke with ecstasy; deeply, this enlightenment had delighted him. Oh, was not all suffering time, were not all forms of tormenting oneself and being afraid time, was not everything hard, everything hostile in the world gone and overcome as soon as one had overcome time, as soon as time would have been put out of existence by one's thoughts? In ecstatic delight, he had spoken, but Vasudeva smiled at him brightly and nodded in confirmation; silently he nodded, brushed his hand over Siddhartha's shoulder, turned back to his work.

And once again, when the river had just increased its flow in the rainy season and made a powerful noise, then said Siddhartha: "Isn't it so, oh friend, the river has many voices, very many voices? Hasn't it the voice of a king, and of a warrior, and of a bull, and of a bird of the night, and of a woman giving birth, and of a sighing man, and a thousand other voices more?"

"So it is," Vasudeva nodded, "all voices of the creatures are in its voice."

"And do you know," Siddhartha continued, "what word it speaks, when you succeed in hearing all of its ten thousand voices at once?"

Happily, Vasudeva's face was smiling, he bent over to Siddhartha and spoke the holy Om into his ear. And this had been the very thing which Siddhartha had also been hearing.

And time after time, his smile became more similar to the ferryman's, became almost just as bright, almost just as throughly glowing with bliss, just as shining out of thousand small wrinkles, just as alike to a child's, just as alike to an old man's. Many travellers, seeing the two ferrymen, thought they were brothers. Often, they sat in the evening together by the bank on the log, said nothing and both listened to the water, which was no water to them, but the voice of life, the voice of what exists, of what is eternally taking shape. And it happened from time to time that both, when listening to the river, thought of the same things, of a conversation from the day before yesterday, of one of their travellers, the face and fate of whom had occupied their thoughts, of death, of their childhood, and that they both in the same moment, when the river had been saying something good to them, looked at each other, both thinking precisely the same thing, both delighted about the same answer to the same question.

There was something about this ferry and the two ferrymen which was transmitted to others, which many of the travellers felt. It happened occasionally that a traveller, after having looked at the face of one of the ferrymen, started to tell the story of his life, told about pains, confessed evil things, asked for comfort and advice. It happened occasionally that someone asked for permission to stay for a night with them to listen to the river. It also happened that curious people came, who had been told that there were two wise men, or sorcerers, or holy men living by that ferry. The curious people asked many questions, but they got no answers, and they found neither sorcerers nor wise men, they only found two friendly little old men, who seemed to be mute and to have become a bit strange and gaga. And the curious people laughed and were discussing how foolishly and gullibly the common people were spreading such empty rumours.

The years passed by, and nobody counted them. Then, at one time, monks came by on a pilgrimage, followers of Gotama, the Buddha, who were asking to be ferried across the river, and by them the ferrymen were told that they were most hurriedly walking back to their great teacher, for the news had spread the exalted one was deadly sick and would soon die his last human death, in order to become one with the salvation. It was not long, until a new flock of monks came along on their pilgrimage, and another one, and the monks as well as most of the other travellers and people walking through the land spoke of nothing else than of Gotama and his impending death. And as people are flocking from everywhere and from all sides, when they are going to war or to the coronation of a king, and are gathering like ants in droves, thus they flocked, like being drawn on by a magic spell, to where the great Buddha was awaiting his death, where the huge event was to take place and the great perfected one of an era was to become one with the glory.

Often, Siddhartha thought in those days of the dying wise man, the great teacher, whose voice had admonished nations and had awoken hundreds of thousands, whose voice he had also once heard, whose holy face he had also once seen with respect. Kindly, he thought of him, saw his path to perfection before his eyes, and remembered with a smile those words which he had once, as a young man, said to him, the exalted one. They had been, so it seemed to him, proud and precocious words; with a smile, he remembered them. For a long time he knew that there was nothing standing between Gotama and him any more, though he was still unable to accept his teachings. No, there was no teaching a truly searching person, someone who truly wanted to find, could accept. But he who had found, he could approve of any teachings, every path, every goal, there was nothing standing between him and all the other thousand any more who lived in that what is eternal, who breathed what is divine.

On one of these days, when so many went on a pilgrimage to the dying Buddha, Kamala also went to him, who used to be the most beautiful of the courtesans. A long time ago, she had retired from her previous life, had given her garden to the monks of Gotama as a gift, had taken her refuge in the teachings, was among the friends and benefactors of the pilgrims. Together with Siddhartha the boy, her son, she had gone on her way due to the news of the near death of Gotama, in simple clothes, on foot. With her little son, she was travelling by the river; but the boy had soon grown tired, desired to go back home, desired to rest, desired to eat, became disobedient and started whining.

Kamala often had to take a rest with him, he was accustomed to having his way against her, she had to feed him, had to comfort him, had to scold him. He did not comprehend why he had to to go on this exhausting and sad pilgrimage with his mother, to an unknown place, to a stranger, who was holy and about to die. So what if he died, how did this concern the boy?

The pilgrims were getting close to Vasudeva's ferry, when little Siddhartha once again forced his mother to rest. She, Kamala herself, had also become tired, and while the boy was chewing a banana, she crouched down on the ground, closed her eyes a bit, and rested. But suddenly, she uttered a wailing scream, the boy looked at her in fear and saw her face having grown pale from horror; and from under her dress, a small, black snake fled, by which Kamala had been bitten.

Hurriedly, they now both ran along the path, in order to reach people, and got near to the ferry, there Kamala collapsed, and was not able to go any further. But the boy started crying miserably, only interrupting it to kiss and hug his mother, and she also joined his loud screams for help, until the sound reached Vasudeva's ears, who stood at the ferry. Quickly, he came walking, took the woman on his arms, carried her into the boat, the boy ran along, and soon they all reached the hut, were Siddhartha stood by the stove and was just lighting the fire. He looked up and first saw the boy's face, which wondrously reminded him of something, like a warning to remember something he had forgotten. Then he saw Kamala, whom he instantly recognised, though she lay unconscious in the ferryman's arms, and now he knew that it was his own son, whose face had been such a warning reminder to him, and the heart stirred in his chest.

Kamala's wound was washed, but had already turned black and her body was swollen, she was made to drink a healing potion. Her consciousness returned, she lay on Siddhartha's bed in the hut and bent over her stood Siddhartha, who used to love her so much. It seemed like a dream to her; with a smile, she looked at her friend's face; just slowly she, realized her situation, remembered the bite, called timidly for the boy.

"He's with you, don't worry," said Siddhartha.

Kamala looked into his eyes. She spoke with a heavy tongue, paralysed by the poison. "You've become old, my dear," she said, "you've become gray. But you are like the young Samana, who at one time came without clothes, with dusty feet, to me into the garden. You are much more like him, than you were like him at that time when you had left me and Kamaswami. In the eyes, you're like him, Siddhartha. Alas, I have also grown old, old—could you still recognise me?"

Siddhartha smiled: "Instantly, I recognised you, Kamala, my dear."

Kamala pointed to her boy and said: "Did you recognise him as well? He is your son."

Her eyes became confused and fell shut. The boy wept, Siddhartha took him on his knees, let him weep, petted his hair, and at the sight of the child's face, a Brahman prayer came to his mind, which he had learned a long time ago, when he had been a little boy himself. Slowly, with a singing voice, he started to speak; from his past and childhood, the words came flowing to him. And with that singsong, the boy became calm, was only now and then uttering a sob and fell asleep. Siddhartha placed him on Vasudeva's bed. Vasudeva stood by the stove and cooked rice. Siddhartha gave him a look, which he returned with a smile.

"She'll die," Siddhartha said quietly.

Vasudeva nodded; over his friendly face ran the light of the stove's fire.

Once again, Kamala returned to consciousness. Pain distorted her face, Siddhartha's eyes read the suffering on her mouth, on her pale cheeks. Quietly, he read it, attentively, waiting, his mind becoming one with her suffering. Kamala felt it, her gaze sought his eyes.

Looking at him, she said: "Now I see that your eyes have changed as well. They've become completely different. By what do I still recognise that you're Siddhartha? It's you, and it's not you."

Siddhartha said nothing, quietly his eyes looked at hers.

"You have achieved it?" she asked. "You have found peace?"

He smiled and placed his hand on hers.

"I'm seeing it," she said, "I'm seeing it. I too will find peace."

"You have found it," Siddhartha spoke in a whisper.

Kamala never stopped looking into his eyes. She thought about her pilgrimage to Gotama, which wanted to take, in order to see the face of the perfected one, to breathe his peace, and she thought that she had now found him in his place, and that it was good, just as good, as if she had seen the other one. She wanted to tell this to him, but the tongue no longer obeyed her will. Without speaking, she looked at him, and he saw the life fading from her eyes. When the final pain filled her eyes and made them grow dim, when the final shiver ran through her limbs, his finger closed her eyelids.

For a long time, he sat and looked at her peacefully dead face. For a long time, he observed her mouth, her old, tired mouth, with those lips, which had become thin, and he remembered, that he used to, in the spring of his years, compare this mouth with a freshly cracked fig. For a long time, he sat, read in the pale face, in the tired wrinkles, filled himself with this sight, saw his own face lying in the same manner, just as white, just as quenched out, and saw at the same time his face and hers being young, with red lips, with fiery eyes, and the feeling of this both being present and at the same time real, the feeling of eternity, completely filled every aspect of his being. Deeply he felt, more deeply than ever before, in this hour, the indestructibility of every life, the eternity of every moment.

When he rose, Vasudeva had prepared rice for him. But Siddhartha did not eat. In the stable, where their goat stood, the two old men prepared beds of straw for themselves, and Vasudeva lay himself down to sleep. But Siddhartha went outside and sat this night before the hut, listening to the river, surrounded by the past, touched and encircled by all times of his life at the same time. But occasionally, he rose, stepped to the door of the hut and listened, whether the boy was sleeping.

Early in the morning, even before the sun could be seen, Vasudeva came out of the stable and walked over to his friend.

"You haven't slept," he said.

"No, Vasudeva. I sat here, I was listening to the river. A lot it has told me, deeply it has filled me with the healing thought, with the thought of oneness."

"You've experienced suffering, Siddhartha, but I see: no sadness has entered your heart."

"No, my dear, how should I be sad? I, who have been rich and happy, have become even richer and happier now. My son has been given to me."

"Your son shall be welcome to me as well. But now, Siddhartha, let's get to work, there is much to be done. Kamala has died on the same bed, on which my wife had died a long time ago. Let us also build Kamala's funeral pile on the same hill on which I had then built my wife's funeral pile."

While the boy was still asleep, they built the funeral pile.

# THE SON

Timid and weeping, the boy had attended his mother's funeral; gloomy and shy, he had listened to Siddhartha, who greeted him as his son and welcomed him at his place in Vasudeva's hut. Pale, he sat for many days by the hill of the dead, did not want to eat, gave no open look, did not open his heart, met his fate with resistance and denial.

Siddhartha spared him and let him do as he pleased, he honoured his mourning. Siddhartha understood that his son did not know him, that he could not love him like a father. Slowly, he also saw and understood that the eleven-year-old was a pampered boy, a mother's boy, and that he had grown up in the habits of rich people, accustomed to finer food, to a soft bed, accustomed to giving orders to servants. Siddhartha understood that the mourning, pampered child could not suddenly and willingly be content with a life among strangers and in poverty. He did not force him, he did many a chore for him, always picked the best piece of the meal for him. Slowly, he hoped to win him over, by friendly patience.

Rich and happy, he had called himself, when the boy had come to him. Since time had passed on in the meantime, and the boy remained a stranger and in a gloomy disposition, since he displayed a proud and stubbornly disobedient heart, did not want to do any work, did not pay his respect to the old men, stole from Vasudeva's fruit-trees, then Siddhartha began to understand that his son had not brought him happiness and peace, but suffering and worry. But he loved him, and he preferred the suffering and worries of love over happiness and joy without the boy. Since young Siddhartha was in the hut, the old men had split the work. Vasudeva had again taken on the job of the ferryman all by himself, and Siddhartha, in order to be with his son, did the work in the hut and the field.

For a long time, for long months, Siddhartha waited for his son to understand him, to accept his love, to perhaps reciprocate it. For long months, Vasudeva waited, watching, waited and said nothing. One day, when Siddhartha the younger had once again tormented his father very much with spite and an unsteadiness in his wishes and had broken both of his rice-bowls, Vasudeva took in the evening his friend aside and talked to him.

"Pardon me." he said, "from a friendly heart, I'm talking to you. I'm seeing that you are tormenting yourself, I'm seeing that you're in grief. Your son, my dear, is worrying you, and he is also worrying me. That young bird is accustomed to a different life, to a different nest. He has not, like you, ran away from riches and the city, being disgusted and fed up with it; against his will, he had to leave all this behind. I asked the river, oh friend, many times I have asked it. But the river laughs, it laughs at me, it laughs at you and me, and is shaking with laughter at out foolishness. Water wants to join water, youth wants to join youth, your son is not in the place where he can prosper. You too should ask the river; you too should listen to it!"

Troubled, Siddhartha looked into his friendly face, in the many wrinkles of which there was incessant cheerfulness.

"How could I part with him?" he said quietly, ashamed. "Give me some more time, my dear! See, I'm fighting for him, I'm seeking to win his heart, with love and with friendly patience I intent to capture it. One day, the river shall also talk to him, he also is called upon."

Vasudeva's smile flourished more warmly. "Oh yes, he too is called upon, he too is of the eternal life. But do we, you and me, know what he is called upon to do, what path to take, what actions to perform, what pain to endure? Not a small one, his pain will be; after all, his heart is proud and hard, people like this have to suffer a lot, err a lot, do much injustice, burden themselves with much sin. Tell me, my dear: you're not taking control of your son's upbringing? You don't force him? You don't beat him? You don't punish him?"

"No, Vasudeva, I don't do anything of this."

"I knew it. You don't force him, don't beat him, don't give him orders, because you know that 'soft' is stronger than 'hard', Water stronger than rocks, love stronger than force. Very good, I praise you. But aren't you mistaken in thinking that you wouldn't force him, wouldn't punish him? Don't you shackle him with your love? Don't you make him feel inferior every day, and don't you make it even harder on him with your kindness and patience? Don't you force him, the arrogant and pampered boy, to live in a hut with two old banana-eaters, to whom even rice is a delicacy, whose thoughts can't be his, whose hearts are old and quiet and beats in a different pace than his? Isn't forced, isn't he punished by all this?"

Troubled, Siddhartha looked to the ground. Quietly, he asked: "What do you think should I do?"

Quoth Vasudeva: "Bring him into the city, bring him into his mother's house, there'll still be servants around, give him to them. And when there aren't any around any more, bring him to a teacher, not for the teachings' sake, but so that he shall be among other boys, and among girls, and in the world which is his own. Have you never thought of this?"

"You're seeing into my heart," Siddhartha spoke sadly. "Often, I have thought of this. But look, how shall I put him, who had no tender heart anyhow, into this world? Won't he become exuberant, won't he lose himself to pleasure and power, won't he repeat all of his father's mistakes, won't he perhaps get entirely lost in Sansara?"

Brightly, the ferryman's smile lit up; softly, he touched Siddhartha's arm and said: "Ask the river about it, my friend! Hear it laugh about it! Would you actually believe that you had committed your foolish acts in order to spare your son from committing them too? And could you in any way protect your son from Sansara? How could you? By means of teachings, prayer, admonition? My dear, have you entirely forgotten that story, that story containing so many lessons, that story about Siddhartha, a Brahman's son, which you once told me here on this very spot? Who has kept the Samana Siddhartha safe from Sansara, from sin, from greed, from foolishness? Were his father's religious devotion, his teachers warnings, his own knowledge, his own search able to keep him safe? Which father, which teacher had been able to protect him from living his life for himself, from soiling himself with life, from burdening himself with guilt, from drinking the bitter drink for himself, from finding his path for himself? Would you think, my dear, anybody might perhaps be spared from taking this path? That perhaps your little son would be spared, because you love him, because you would like to keep him from suffering and pain and disappointment? But even if you would die ten times for him, you would not be able to take the slightest part of his destiny upon yourself."

Never before, Vasudeva had spoken so many words. Kindly, Siddhartha thanked him, went troubled into the hut, could not sleep for a long time. Vasudeva had told him nothing, he had not already thought and known for himself. But this was a knowledge he could not act upon, stronger than the knowledge was his love for the boy, stronger was his tenderness, his fear to lose him. Had he ever lost his heart so much to something, had he ever loved any person thus, thus blindly, thus sufferingly, thus unsuccessfully, and yet thus happily?

Siddhartha could not heed his friend's advice, he could not give up the boy. He let the boy give him orders, he let him disregard him. He said nothing and waited; daily, he began the mute struggle of friendliness, the silent war of patience. Vasudeva also said nothing and waited, friendly, knowing, patient. They were both masters of patience.

At one time, when the boy's face reminded him very much of Kamala, Siddhartha suddenly had to think of a line which Kamala a long time ago, in the days of their youth, had once said to him. "You cannot love," she had said to him, and he had agreed with her and had compared himself with a star, while comparing the childlike people with falling leaves, and nevertheless he had also sensed an accusation in that line. Indeed, he had never been able to lose or devote himself completely to another person, to forget himself, to commit foolish acts for the love of another person; never he had been able to do this, and this was, as it had seemed to him at that time, the great distinction which set him apart from the childlike people. But now, since his son was here, now he, Siddhartha, had also become completely a childlike person, suffering for the sake of another person, loving another person, lost to a love, having become a fool on account of love. Now he too felt, late, once in his lifetime, this strongest and strangest of all passions, suffered from it, suffered miserably, and was nevertheless in bliss, was nevertheless renewed in one respect, enriched by one thing.

He did sense very well that this love, this blind love for his son, was a passion, something very human, that it was Sansara, a murky source, dark waters. Nevertheless, he felt at the same time, it was not worthless, it was necessary, came from the essence of his own being. This pleasure also had to be atoned for, this pain also had to be endured, these foolish acts also had to be committed.

Through all this, the son let him commit his foolish acts, let him court for his affection, let him humiliate himself every day by giving in to his moods. This father had nothing which would have delighted him and nothing which he would have feared. He was a good man, this father, a good, kind, soft man, perhaps a very devout man, perhaps a saint, all these there no attributes which could win the boy over. He was bored by this father, who kept him prisoner here in this miserable hut of his, he was bored by him, and for him to answer every naughtiness with a smile, every insult with friendliness, every viciousness with kindness, this very thing was the hated trick of this old sneak. Much more the boy would have liked it if he had been threatened by him, if he had been abused by him.

A day came, when what young Siddhartha had on his mind came bursting forth, and he openly turned against his father. The latter had given him a task, he had told him to gather brushwood. But the boy did not leave the hut, in stubborn disobedience and rage he stayed where he was, thumped on the ground with his feet, clenched his fists, and screamed in a powerful outburst his hatred and contempt into his father's face.

"Get the brushwood for yourself!" he shouted foaming at the mouth, "I'm not your servant. I do know, that you won't hit me, you don't dare; I do know, that you constantly want to punish me and put me down with your religious devotion and your indulgence. You want me to become like you, just as devout, just as soft, just as wise! But I, listen up, just to make you suffer, I rather want to become a highway-robber and murderer, and go to hell, than to become like you! I hate you, you're not my father, and if you've ten times been my mother's fornicator!"

Rage and grief boiled over in him, foamed at the father in a hundred savage and evil words. Then the boy ran away and only returned late at night.

But the next morning, he had disappeared. What had also disappeared was a small basket, woven out of bast of two colours, in which the ferrymen kept those copper and silver coins which they received as a fare. The boat had also disappeared, Siddhartha saw it lying by the opposite bank. The boy had ran away.

"I must follow him," said Siddhartha, who had been shivering with grief since those ranting speeches, the boy had made yesterday. "A child can't go through the forest all alone. He'll perish. We must build a raft, Vasudeva, to get over the water."

"We will build a raft," said Vasudeva, "to get our boat back, which the boy has taken away. But him, you shall let run along, my friend, he is no child any more, he knows how to get around. He's looking for the path to the city, and he is right, don't forget that. He's doing what you've failed to do yourself. He's taking care of himself, he's taking his course. Alas, Siddhartha, I see you suffering, but you're suffering a pain at which one would like to laugh, at which you'll soon laugh for yourself."

Siddhartha did not answer. He already held the axe in his hands and began to make a raft of bamboo, and Vasudeva helped him to tied the canes together with ropes of grass. Then they crossed over, drifted far off their course, pulled the raft upriver on the opposite bank.

"Why did you take the axe along?" asked Siddhartha.

Vasudeva said: "It might have been possible that the oar of our boat got lost."

But Siddhartha knew what his friend was thinking. He thought, the boy would have thrown away or broken the oar in order to get even and in order to keep them from following him. And in fact, there was no oar left in the boat. Vasudeva pointed to the bottom of the boat and looked at his friend with a smile, as if he wanted to say: "Don't you see what your son is trying to tell you? Don't you see that he doesn't want to be followed?" But he did not say this in words. He started making a new oar. But Siddhartha bid his farewell, to look for the run-away. Vasudeva did not stop him.

When Siddhartha had already been walking through the forest for a long time, the thought occurred to him that his search was useless. Either, so he thought, the boy was far ahead and had already reached the city, or, if he should still be on his way, he would conceal himself from him, the pursuer. As he continued thinking, he also found that he, on his part, was not worried for his son, that he knew deep inside that he had neither perished nor was in any danger in the forest. Nevertheless, he ran without stopping, no longer to save him, just to satisfy his desire, just to perhaps see him one more time. And he ran up to just outside of the city.

When, near the city, he reached a wide road, he stopped, by the entrance of the beautiful pleasure-garden, which used to belong to Kamala, where he had seen her for the first time in her sedan-chair. The past rose up in his soul, again he saw himself standing there, young, a bearded, naked Samana, the hair full of dust. For a long time, Siddhartha stood there and looked through the open gate into the garden, seeing monks in yellow robes walking among the beautiful trees.

For a long time, he stood there, pondering, seeing images, listening to the story of his life. For a long time, he stood there, looked at the monks, saw young Siddhartha in their place, saw young Kamala walking among the high trees. Clearly, he saw himself being served food and drink by Kamala, receiving his first kiss from her, looking proudly and disdainfully back on his Brahmanism, beginning proudly and full of desire his worldly life. He saw Kamaswami, saw the servants, the orgies, the gamblers with the dice, the musicians, saw Kamala's song-bird in the cage, lived through all this once again, breathed Sansara, was once again old and tired, felt once again disgust, felt once again the wish to annihilate himself, was once again healed by the holy Om.

After having been standing by the gate of the garden for a long time, Siddhartha realised that his desire was foolish, which had made him go up to this place, that he could not help his son, that he was not allowed to cling him. Deeply, he felt the love for the run-away in his heart, like a wound, and he felt at the same time that this wound had not been given to him in order to turn the knife in it, that it had to become a blossom and had to shine.

That this wound did not blossom yet, did not shine yet, at this hour, made him sad. Instead of the desired goal, which had drawn him here following the runaway son, there was now emptiness. Sadly, he sat down, felt something dying in his heart, experienced emptiness, saw no joy any more, no goal. He sat lost in thought and waited. This he had learned by the river, this one thing: waiting, having patience, listening attentively. And he sat and listened, in the dust of the road, listened to his heart, beating tiredly and sadly, waited for a voice. Many an hour he crouched, listening, saw no images any more, fell into emptiness, let himself fall, without seeing a path. And when he felt the wound burning, he silently spoke the Om, filled himself with Om. The monks in the garden saw him, and since he crouched for many hours, and dust was gathering on his gray hair, one of them came to him and placed two bananas in front of him. The old man did not see him.

From this petrified state, he was awoken by a hand touching his shoulder. Instantly, he recognised this touch, this tender, bashful touch, and regained his senses. He rose and greeted Vasudeva, who had followed him. And when he looked into Vasudeva's friendly face, into the small wrinkles, which were as if they were filled with nothing but his smile, into the happy eyes, then he smiled too. Now he saw the bananas lying in front of him, picked them up, gave one to the ferryman, ate the other one himself. After this, he silently went back into the forest with Vasudeva, returned home to the ferry. Neither one talked about what had happened today, neither one mentioned the boy's name, neither one spoke about him running away, neither one spoke about the wound. In the hut, Siddhartha lay down on his bed, and when after a while Vasudeva came to him, to offer him a bowl of coconut-milk, he already found him asleep.

# OM

For a long time, the wound continued to burn. Many a traveller Siddhartha had to ferry across the river who was accompanied by a son or a daughter, and he saw none of them without envying him, without thinking: "So many, so many thousands possess this sweetest of good fortunes—why don't I? Even bad people, even thieves and robbers have children and love them, and are being loved by them, all except for me." Thus simply, thus without reason he now thought, thus similar to the childlike people he had become.

Differently than before, he now looked upon people, less smart, less proud, but instead warmer, more curious, more involved. When he ferried travellers of the ordinary kind, childlike people, businessmen, warriors, women, these people did not seem alien to him as they used to: he understood them, he understood and shared their life, which was not guided by thoughts and insight, but solely by urges and wishes, he felt like them. Though he was near perfection and was bearing his final wound, it still seemed to him as if those childlike people were his brothers, their vanities, desires for possession, and ridiculous aspects were no longer ridiculous to him, became understandable, became lovable, even became worthy of veneration to him. The blind love of a mother for her child, the stupid, blind pride of a conceited father for his only son, the blind, wild desire of a young, vain woman for jewelry and admiring glances from men, all of these urges, all of this childish stuff, all of these simple, foolish, but immensely strong, strongly living, strongly prevailing urges and desires were now no childish notions for Siddhartha any more, he saw people living for their sake, saw them achieving infinitely much for their sake, travelling, conducting wars, suffering infinitely much, bearing infinitely much, and he could love them for it, he saw life, that what is alive, the indestructible, the Brahman in each of their passions, each of their acts. Worthy of love and admiration were these people in their blind loyalty, their blind strength and tenacity. They lacked nothing, there was nothing the knowledgeable one, the thinker, had to put him above them except for one little thing, a single, tiny, small thing: the consciousness, the conscious thought of the oneness of all life. And Siddhartha even doubted in many an hour, whether this knowledge, this thought was to be valued thus highly, whether it might not also perhaps be a childish idea of the thinking people, of the thinking and childlike people. In all other respects, the worldly people were of equal rank to the wise men, were often far superior to them, just as animals too can, after all, in some moments, seem to be superior to humans in their tough, unrelenting performance of what is necessary.

Slowly blossomed, slowly ripened in Siddhartha the realisation, the knowledge, what wisdom actually was, what the goal of his long search was. It was nothing but a readiness of the soul, an ability, a secret art, to think every moment, while living his life, the thought of oneness, to be able to feel and inhale the oneness. Slowly this blossomed in him, was shining back at him from Vasudeva's old, childlike face: harmony, knowledge of the eternal perfection of the world, smiling, oneness.

But the wound still burned, longingly and bitterly Siddhartha thought of his son, nurtured his love and tenderness in his heart, allowed the pain to gnaw at him, committed all foolish acts of love. Not by itself, this flame would go out.

And one day, when the wound burned violently, Siddhartha ferried across the river, driven by a yearning, got off the boat and was willing to go to the city and to look for his son. The river flowed softly and quietly, it was the dry season, but its voice sounded strange: it laughed! It laughed clearly. The river laughed, it laughed brightly and clearly at the old ferryman. Siddhartha stopped, he bent over the water, in order to hear even better, and he saw his face reflected in the quietly moving waters, and in this reflected face there was something, which reminded him, something he had forgotten, and as he thought about it, he found it: this face resembled another face, which he used to know and love and also fear. It resembled his father's face, the Brahman. And he remembered how he, a long time ago, as a young man, had forced his father to let him go to the penitents, how he had bed his farewell to him, how he had gone and had never come back. Had his father not also suffered the same pain for him, which he now suffered for his son? Had his father not long since died, alone, without having seen his son again? Did he not have to expect the same fate for himself? Was it not a comedy, a strange and stupid matter, this repetition, this running around in a fateful circle?

The river laughed. Yes, so it was, everything came back, which had not been suffered and solved up to its end, the same pain was suffered over and over again. But Siddhartha went back into the boat and ferried back to the hut, thinking of his father, thinking of his son, laughed at by the river, at odds with himself, tending towards despair, and not less tending towards laughing along at (?? über) himself and the entire world.

Alas, the wound was not blossoming yet, his heart was still fighting his fate, cheerfulness and victory were not yet shining from his suffering. Nevertheless, he felt hope, and once he had returned to the hut, he felt an undefeatable desire to open up to Vasudeva, to show him everything, the master of listening, to say everything.

Vasudeva was sitting in the hut and weaving a basket. He no longer used the ferry-boat, his eyes were starting to get weak, and not just his eyes; his arms and hands as well. Unchanged and flourishing was only the joy and the cheerful benevolence of his face.

Siddhartha sat down next to the old man, slowly he started talking. What they had never talked about, he now told him of, of his walk to the city, at that time, of the burning wound, of his envy at the sight of happy fathers, of his knowledge of the foolishness of such wishes, of his futile fight against them. He reported everything, he was able to say everything, even the most embarrassing parts, everything could be said, everything shown, everything he could tell. He presented his wound, also told how he fled today, how he ferried across the water, a childish run-away, willing to walk to the city, how the river had laughed.

While he spoke, spoke for a long time, while Vasudeva was listening with a quiet face, Vasudeva's listening gave Siddhartha a stronger sensation than ever before, he sensed how his pain, his fears flowed over to him, how his secret hope flowed over, came back at him from his counterpart. To show his wound to this listener was the same as bathing it in the river, until it had cooled and become one with the river. While he was still speaking, still admitting and confessing, Siddhartha felt more and more that this was no longer Vasudeva, no longer a human being, who was listening to him, that this motionless listener was absorbing his confession into himself like a tree the rain, that this motionless man was the river itself, that he was God himself, that he was the eternal itself. And while Siddhartha stopped thinking of himself and his wound, this realisation of Vasudeva's changed character took possession of him, and the more he felt it and entered into it, the less wondrous it became, the more he realised that everything was in order and natural, that Vasudeva had already been like this for a long time, almost forever, that only he had not quite recognised it, yes, that he himself had almost reached the same state. He felt, that he was now seeing old Vasudeva as the people see the gods, and that this could not last; in his heart, he started bidding his farewell to Vasudeva. Thorough all this, he talked incessantly.

When he had finished talking, Vasudeva turned his friendly eyes, which had grown slightly weak, at him, said nothing, let his silent love and cheerfulness, understanding and knowledge, shine at him. He took Siddhartha's hand, led him to the seat by the bank, sat down with him, smiled at the river.

"You've heard it laugh," he said. "But you haven't heard everything. Let's listen, you'll hear more."

They listened. Softly sounded the river, singing in many voices. Siddhartha looked into the water, and images appeared to him in the moving water: his father appeared, lonely, mourning for his son; he himself appeared, lonely, he also being tied with the bondage of yearning to his distant son; his son appeared, lonely as well, the boy, greedily rushing along the burning course of his young wishes, each one heading for his goal, each one obsessed by the goal, each one suffering. The river sang with a voice of suffering, longingly it sang, longingly, it flowed towards its goal, lamentingly its voice sang.

"Do you hear?" Vasudeva's mute gaze asked. Siddhartha nodded.

"Listen better!" Vasudeva whispered.

Siddhartha made an effort to listen better. The image of his father, his own image, the image of his son merged, Kamala's image also appeared and was dispersed, and the image of Govinda, and other images, and they merged with each other, turned all into the river, headed all, being the river, for the goal, longing, desiring, suffering, and the river's voice sounded full of yearning, full of burning woe, full of unsatisfiable desire. For the goal, the river was heading, Siddhartha saw it hurrying, the river, which consisted of him and his loved ones and of all people, he had ever seen, all of these waves and waters were hurrying, suffering, towards goals, many goals, the waterfall, the lake, the rapids, the sea, and all goals were reached, and every goal was followed by a new one, and the water turned into vapour and rose to the sky, turned into rain and poured down from the sky, turned into a source, a stream, a river, headed forward once again, flowed on once again. But the longing voice had changed. It still resounded, full of suffering, searching, but other voices joined it, voices of joy and of suffering, good and bad voices, laughing and sad ones, a hundred voices, a thousand voices.

Siddhartha listened. He was now nothing but a listener, completely concentrated on listening, completely empty, he felt, that he had now finished learning to listen. Often before, he had heard all this, these many voices in the river, today it sounded new.

Already, he could no longer tell the many voices apart, not the happy ones from the weeping ones, not the ones of children from those of men, they all belonged together, the lamentation of yearning and the laughter of the knowledgeable one, the scream of rage and the moaning of the dying ones, everything was one, everything was intertwined and connected, entangled a thousand times. And everything together, all voices, all goals, all yearning, all suffering, all pleasure, all that was good and evil, all of this together was the world. All of it together was the flow of events, was the music of life. And when Siddhartha was listening attentively to this river, this song of a thousand voices, when he neither listened to the suffering nor the laughter, when he did not tie his soul to any particular voice and submerged his self into it, but when he heard them all, perceived the whole, the oneness, then the great song of the thousand voices consisted of a single word, which was Om: the perfection.

"Do you hear," Vasudeva's gaze asked again.

Brightly, Vasudeva's smile was shining, floating radiantly over all the wrinkles of his old face, as the Om was floating in the air over all the voices of the river. Brightly his smile was shining, when he looked at his friend, and brightly the same smile was now starting to shine on Siddhartha's face as well. His wound blossomed, his suffering was shining, his self had flown into the oneness.

In this hour, Siddhartha stopped fighting his fate, stopped suffering. On his face flourished the cheerfulness of a knowledge, which is no longer opposed by any will, which knows perfection, which is in agreement with the flow of events, with the current of life, full of sympathy for the pain of others, full of sympathy for the pleasure of others, devoted to the flow, belonging to the oneness.

When Vasudeva rose from the seat by the bank, when he looked into Siddhartha's eyes and saw the cheerfulness of the knowledge shining in them, he softly touched his shoulder with his hand, in this careful and tender manner, and said: "I've been waiting for this hour, my dear. Now that it has come, let me leave. For a long time, I've been waiting for this hour; for a long time, I've been Vasudeva the ferryman. Now it's enough. Farewell, hut, farewell, river, farewell, Siddhartha!"

Siddhartha made a deep bow before him who bid his farewell.

"I've known it," he said quietly. "You'll go into the forests?"

"I'm going into the forests, I'm going into the oneness," spoke Vasudeva with a bright smile.

With a bright smile, he left; Siddhartha watched him leaving. With deep joy, with deep solemnity he watched him leave, saw his steps full of peace, saw his head full of lustre, saw his body full of light.

# GOVINDA

Together with other monks, Govinda used to spend the time of rest between pilgrimages in the pleasure-grove, which the courtesan Kamala had given to the followers of Gotama for a gift. He heard talk of an old ferryman, who lived one day's journey away by the river, and who was regarded as a wise man by many. When Govinda went back on his way, he chose the path to the ferry, eager to see the ferryman. Because, though he had lived his entire life by the rules, though he was also looked upon with veneration by the younger monks on account of his age and his modesty, the restlessness and the searching still had not perished from his heart.

He came to the river and asked the old man to ferry him over, and when they got off the boat on the other side, he said to the old man: "You're very good to us monks and pilgrims, you have already ferried many of us across the river. Aren't you too, ferryman, a searcher for the right path?"

Quoth Siddhartha, smiling from his old eyes: "Do you call yourself a searcher, oh venerable one, though you are already of an old in years and are wearing the robe of Gotama's monks?"

"It's true, I'm old," spoke Govinda, "but I haven't stopped searching. Never I'll stop searching, this seems to be my destiny. You too, so it seems to me, have been searching. Would you like to tell me something, oh honourable one?"

Quoth Siddhartha: "What should I possibly have to tell you, oh venerable one? Perhaps that you're searching far too much? That in all that searching, you don't find the time for finding?"

"How come?" asked Govinda.

"When someone is searching," said Siddhartha, "then it might easily happen that the only thing his eyes still see is that what he searches for, that he is unable to find anything, to let anything enter his mind, because he always thinks of nothing but the object of his search, because he has a goal, because he is obsessed by the goal. Searching means: having a goal. But finding means: being free, being open, having no goal. You, oh venerable one, are perhaps indeed a searcher, because, striving for your goal, there are many things you don't see, which are directly in front of your eyes."

"I don't quite understand yet," asked Govinda, "what do you mean by this?"

Quoth Siddhartha: "A long time ago, oh venerable one, many years ago, you've once before been at this river and have found a sleeping man by the river, and have sat down with him to guard his sleep. But, oh Govinda, you did not recognise the sleeping man."

Astonished, as if he had been the object of a magic spell, the monk looked into the ferryman's eyes.

"Are you Siddhartha?" he asked with a timid voice. "I wouldn't have recognised you this time as well! From my heart, I'm greeting you, Siddhartha; from my heart, I'm happy to see you once again! You've changed a lot, my friend.—And so you've now become a ferryman?"

In a friendly manner, Siddhartha laughed. "A ferryman, yes. Many people, Govinda, have to change a lot, have to wear many a robe, I am one of those, my dear. Be welcome, Govinda, and spend the night in my hut."

Govinda stayed the night in the hut and slept on the bed which used to be Vasudeva's bed. Many questions he posed to the friend of his youth, many things Siddhartha had to tell him from his life.

When in the next morning the time had come to start the day's journey, Govinda said, not without hesitation, these words: "Before I'll continue on my path, Siddhartha, permit me to ask one more question. Do you have a teaching? Do you have a faith, or a knowledge, you follow, which helps you to live and to do right?"

Quoth Siddhartha: "You know, my dear, that I already as a young man, in those days when we lived with the penitents in the forest, started to distrust teachers and teachings and to turn my back to them. I have stuck with this. Nevertheless, I have had many teachers since then. A beautiful courtesan has been my teacher for a long time, and a rich merchant was my teacher, and some gamblers with dice. Once, even a follower of Buddha, travelling on foot, has been my teacher; he sat with me when I had fallen asleep in the forest, on the pilgrimage. I've also learned from him, I'm also grateful to him, very grateful. But most of all, I have learned here from this river and from my predecessor, the ferryman Vasudeva. He was a very simple person, Vasudeva, he was no thinker, but he knew what is necessary just as well as Gotama, he was a perfect man, a saint."

Govinda said: "Still, oh Siddhartha, you love a bit to mock people, as it seems to me. I believe in you and know that you haven't followed a teacher. But haven't you found something by yourself, though you've found no teachings, you still found certain thoughts, certain insights, which are your own and which help you to live? If you would like to tell me some of these, you would delight my heart."

Quoth Siddhartha: "I've had thoughts, yes, and insight, again and again. Sometimes, for an hour or for an entire day, I have felt knowledge in me, as one would feel life in one's heart. There have been many thoughts, but it would be hard for me to convey them to you. Look, my dear Govinda, this is one of my thoughts, which I have found: wisdom cannot be passed on. Wisdom which a wise man tries to pass on to someone always sounds like foolishness."

"Are you kidding?" asked Govinda.

"I'm not kidding. I'm telling you what I've found. Knowledge can be conveyed, but not wisdom. It can be found, it can be lived, it is possible to be carried by it, miracles can be performed with it, but it cannot be expressed in words and taught. This was what I, even as a young man, sometimes suspected, what has driven me away from the teachers. I have found a thought, Govinda, which you'll again regard as a joke or foolishness, but which is my best thought. It says: The opposite of every truth is just as true! That's like this: any truth can only be expressed and put into words when it is one-sided. Everything is one-sided which can be thought with thoughts and said with words, it's all one-sided, all just one half, all lacks completeness, roundness, oneness. When the exalted Gotama spoke in his teachings of the world, he had to divide it into Sansara and Nirvana, into deception and truth, into suffering and salvation. It cannot be done differently, there is no other way for him who wants to teach. But the world itself, what exists around us and inside of us, is never one-sided. A person or an act is never entirely Sansara or entirely Nirvana, a person is never entirely holy or entirely sinful. It does really seem like this, because we are subject to deception, as if time was something real. Time is not real, Govinda, I have experienced this often and often again. And if time is not real, then the gap which seems to be between the world and the eternity, between suffering and blissfulness, between evil and good, is also a deception."

"How come?" asked Govinda timidly.

"Listen well, my dear, listen well! The sinner, which I am and which you are, is a sinner, but in times to come he will be Brahma again, he will reach the Nirvana, will be

Buddha—and now see: these 'times to come' are a deception, are only a parable! The sinner is not on his way to become a Buddha, he is not in the process of developing, though our capacity for thinking does not know how else to picture these things. No, within the sinner is now and today already the future Buddha, his future is already all there, you have to worship in him, in you, in everyone the Buddha which is coming into being, the possible, the hidden Buddha. The world, my friend Govinda, is not imperfect, or on a slow path towards perfection: no, it is perfect in every moment, all sin already carries the divine forgiveness in itself, all small children already have the old person in themselves, all infants already have death, all dying people the eternal life. It is not possible for any person to see how far another one has already progressed on his path; in the robber and dice-gambler, the Buddha is waiting; in the Brahman, the robber is waiting. In deep meditation, there is the possibility to put time out of existence, to see all life which was, is, and will be as if it was simultaneous, and there everything is good, everything is perfect, everything is Brahman. Therefore, I see whatever exists as good, death is to me like life, sin like holiness, wisdom like foolishness, everything has to be as it is, everything only requires my consent, only my willingness, my loving agreement, to be good for me, to do nothing but work for my benefit, to be unable to ever harm me. I have experienced on my body and on my soul that I needed sin very much, I needed lust, the desire for possessions, vanity, and needed the most shameful despair, in order to learn how to give up all resistance, in order to learn how to love the world, in order to stop comparing it to some world I wished, I imagined, some kind of perfection I had made up, but to leave it as it is and to love it and to enjoy being a part of it.—These, oh Govinda, are some of the thoughts which have come into my mind."

Siddhartha bent down, picked up a stone from the ground, and weighed it in his hand.

"This here," he said playing with it, "is a stone, and will, after a certain time, perhaps turn into soil, and will turn from soil into a plant or animal or human being. In the past, I would have said: This stone is just a stone, it is worthless, it belongs to the world of the Maja; but because it might be able to become also a human being and a spirit in the cycle of transformations, therefore I also grant it importance. Thus, I would perhaps have thought in the past. But today I think: this stone is a stone, it is also animal, it is also god, it is also Buddha, I do not venerate and love it because it could turn into this or that, but rather because it is already and always everything— and it is this very fact, that it is a stone, that it appears to me now and today as a stone, this is why I love it and see worth and purpose in each of its veins and cavities, in the yellow, in the gray, in the hardness, in the sound it makes when I knock at it, in the dryness or wetness of its surface. There are stones which feel like oil or soap, and others like leaves, others like sand, and every one is special and prays the Om in its own way, each one is Brahman, but simultaneously and just as much it is a stone, is oily or juicy, and this is this very fact which I like and regard as wonderful and worthy of worship.—But let me speak no more of this. The words are not good for the secret meaning, everything always becomes a bit different, as soon as it is put into words, gets distorted a bit, a bit silly— yes, and this is also very good, and I like it a lot, I also very much agree with this, that this what is one man's treasure and wisdom always sounds like foolishness to another person."

Govinda listened silently.

"Why have you told me this about the stone?" he asked hesitantly after a pause.

"I did it without any specific intention. Or perhaps what I meant was, that love this very stone, and the river, and all these things we are looking at and from which we can learn. I can love a stone, Govinda, and also a tree or a piece of bark. This are things, and things can be loved. But I cannot love words. Therefore, teachings are no good for me, they have no hardness, no softness, no colours, no edges, no smell, no taste, they have nothing but words. Perhaps it are these which keep you from finding peace, perhaps it are the many words. Because salvation and virtue as well, Sansara and Nirvana as well, are mere words, Govinda. There is no thing which would be Nirvana; there is just the word Nirvana."

Quoth Govinda: "Not just a word, my friend, is Nirvana. It is a thought."

Siddhartha continued: "A thought, it might be so. I must confess to you, my dear: I don't differentiate much between thoughts and words. To be honest, I also have no high opinion of thoughts. I have a better opinion of things. Here on this ferry-boat, for instance, a man has been my predecessor and teacher, a holy man, who has for many years simply believed in the river, nothing else. He had noticed that the river's spoke to him, he learned from it, it educated and taught him, the river seemed to be a god to him, for many years he did not know that every wind, every cloud, every bird, every beetle was just as divine and knows just as much and can teach just as much as the worshipped river. But when this holy man went into the forests, he knew everything, knew more than you and me, without teachers, without books, only because he had believed in the river."

Govinda said: "But is that what you call `things', actually something real, something which has existence? Isn't it just a deception of the Maja, just an image and illusion? Your stone, your tree, your river— are they actually a reality?"

"This too," spoke Siddhartha, "I do not care very much about. Let the things be illusions or not, after all I would then also be an illusion, and thus they are always like me. This is what makes them so dear and worthy of veneration for me: they are like me. Therefore, I can love them. And this is now a teaching you will laugh about: love, oh Govinda, seems to me to be the most important thing of all. To thoroughly understand the world, to explain it, to despise it, may be the thing great thinkers do. But I'm only interested in being able to love the world, not to despise it, not to hate it and me, to be able to look upon it and me and all beings with love and admiration and great respect."

"This I understand," spoke Govinda. "But this very thing was discovered by the exalted one to be a deception. He commands benevolence, clemency, sympathy, tolerance, but not love; he forbade us to tie our heart in love to earthly things."

"I know it," said Siddhartha; his smile shone golden. "I know it, Govinda. And behold, with this we are right in the middle of the thicket of opinions, in the dispute about words. For I cannot deny, my words of love are in a contradiction, a seeming contradiction with Gotama's words. For this very reason, I distrust in words so much, for I know, this contradiction is a deception. I know that I am in agreement with Gotama. How should he not know love, he, who has discovered all elements of human existence in their transitoriness, in their meaninglessness, and yet loved people thus much, to use a long, laborious life only to help them, to teach them! Even with him, even with your great teacher, I prefer the thing over the words, place more importance on his acts and life than on his speeches, more on the gestures of his hand than his opinions. Not in his speech, not in his thoughts, I see his greatness, only in his actions, in his life."

For a long time, the two old men said nothing. Then spoke Govinda, while bowing for a farewell: "I thank you, Siddhartha, for telling me some of your thoughts. They are partially strange thoughts, not all have been instantly understandable to me. This being as it may, I thank you, and I wish you to have calm days."

(But secretly he thought to himself: This Siddhartha is a bizarre person, he expresses bizarre thoughts, his teachings sound foolish. So differently sound the exalted one's pure teachings, clearer, purer, more comprehensible, nothing strange, foolish, or silly is contained in them. But different from his thoughts seemed to me Siddhartha's hands and feet, his eyes, his forehead, his breath, his smile, his greeting, his walk. Never again, after our exalted Gotama has become one with the Nirvana, never since then have I met a person of whom I felt: this is a holy man! Only him, this Siddhartha, I have found to be like this. May his teachings be strange, may his words sound foolish; out of his gaze and his hand, his skin and his hair, out of every part of him shines a purity, shines a calmness, shines a cheerfulness and mildness and holiness, which I have seen in no other person since the final death of our exalted teacher.)

As Govinda thought like this, and there was a conflict in his heart, he once again bowed to Siddhartha, drawn by love. Deeply he bowed to him who was calmly sitting.

"Siddhartha," he spoke, "we have become old men. It is unlikely for one of us to see the other again in this incarnation. I see, beloved, that you have found peace. I confess that I haven't found it. Tell me, oh honourable one, one more word, give me something on my way which I can grasp, which I can understand! Give me something to be with me on my path. It it often hard, my path, often dark, Siddhartha."

Siddhartha said nothing and looked at him with the ever unchanged, quiet smile. Govinda stared at his face, with fear, with yearning, suffering, and the eternal search was visible in his look, eternal not-finding.

Siddhartha saw it and smiled.

"Bent down to me!" he whispered quietly in Govinda's ear. "Bend down to me! Like this, even closer! Very close! Kiss my forehead, Govinda!"

But while Govinda with astonishment, and yet drawn by great love and expectation, obeyed his words, bent down closely to him and touched his forehead with his lips, something miraculous happened to him. While his thoughts were still dwelling on Siddhartha's wondrous words, while he was still struggling in vain and with reluctance to think away time, to imagine Nirvana and Sansara as one, while even a certain contempt for the words of his friend was fighting in him against an immense love and veneration, this happened to him:

He no longer saw the face of his friend Siddhartha, instead he saw other faces, many, a long sequence, a flowing river of faces, of hundreds, of thousands, which all came and disappeared, and yet all seemed to be there simultaneously, which all constantly changed and renewed themselves, and which were still all Siddhartha. He saw the face of a fish, a carp, with an infinitely painfully opened mouth, the face of a dying fish, with fading eyes —he saw the face of a new-born child, red and full of wrinkles, distorted from crying— he saw the face of a murderer, he saw him plunging a knife into the body of another person—he saw, in the same second, this criminal in bondage, kneeling and his head being chopped off by the executioner with one blow of his sword—he saw the bodies of men and women, naked in positions and cramps of frenzied love—he saw corpses stretched out, motionless, cold, void— he saw the heads of animals, of boars, of crocodiles, of elephants, of bulls, of birds—he saw gods, saw Krishna, saw Agni—he saw all of these figures and faces in a thousand relationships with one another, each one helping the other, loving it, hating it, destroying it, giving re-birth to it, each one was a will to die, a passionately painful confession of transitoriness, and yet none of them died, each one only transformed, was always re-born, received evermore a new face, without any time having passed between the one and the other face—and all of these figures and faces rested, flowed, generated themselves, floated along and merged with each other, and they were all constantly covered by something thin, without individuality of its own, but yet existing, like a thin glass or ice, like a transparent skin, a shell or mold or mask of water, and this mask was smiling, and this mask was Siddhartha's smiling face, which he, Govinda, in this very same moment touched with his lips. And, Govinda saw it like this, this smile of the mask, this smile of oneness above the flowing forms, this smile of simultaneousness above the thousand births and deaths, this smile of Siddhartha was precisely the same, was precisely of the same kind as the quiet, delicate, impenetrable, perhaps benevolent, perhaps mocking, wise, thousand-fold smile of Gotama, the Buddha, as he had seen it himself with great respect a hundred times. Like this, Govinda knew, the perfected ones are smiling.

Not knowing any more whether time existed, whether the vision had lasted a second or a hundred years, not knowing any more whether there existed a Siddhartha, a Gotama, a me and a you, feeling in his innermost self as if he had been wounded by a divine arrow, the injury of which tasted sweet, being enchanted and dissolved in his innermost self, Govinda still stood for a little while bent over Siddhartha's quiet face, which he had just kissed, which had just been the scene of all manifestations, all transformations, all existence. The face was unchanged, after under its surface the depth of the thousandfoldness had closed up again, he smiled silently, smiled quietly and softly, perhaps very benevolently, perhaps very mockingly, precisely as he used to smile, the exalted one.

Deeply, Govinda bowed; tears he knew nothing of, ran down his old face; like a fire burnt the feeling of the most intimate love, the humblest veneration in his heart. Deeply, he bowed, touching the ground, before him who was sitting motionlessly, whose smile reminded him of everything he had ever loved in his life, what had ever been valuable and holy to him in his life.